Beyond the Stars

A Science Fiction and Fantasy Short Story Collection

C.I. Chevron

CYPRESS KNOLL
PRESS

Cypress Knoll Press

Cookville, TX

This book is a work of fiction. Names, characters, businesses, organizations, places, events and incidents either are the product of the author's imagination or are used fictitiously. Any resemblance to actual persons, living or dead, events, or locales is entirely coincidental.

For information contact; address www.CIChevron.com

Book and Cover design by Em-Cat Designs

ISBN: 978-1-7335913-3-1

First Edition: May 2019

CONTENTS

Aknowledgements

This book could not have happened without all those hardworking people who run and judge the various short story contests all over the world. They are never paid enough for their time and effort, but the value and encouragement (as painful as it is sometimes) to the fledging writer is tremendous.

Here, dear reader, you will find the gamut of my stories from when I first starting writing to now. Some are award winners, others honorable mentions, still others never placed anywhere but I love them, and I hope you do too.

Enjoy.

C. I. Chevron

A Walk in the Park with Death and Winter

First Place, NETWO Short Story Contest, 2013

I AM WINTER AND TONIGHT I DANCE WITH DEATH
Or rather, he stalks, and I dance. I skate over puddles and turn them to ice. I twirl, and leap, and twist, unfurling his cloak and admiring the glitter of snowflakes against its inky color.

An old man sleeps under a bridge.

With a flick of my hand the newspaper over his face floats towards the river. Death steps forward as I lean down and kiss his lips blue and his eyelids with ice. His beauty stirs my soul. So many times, Death and I have walked together over battlefields and disasters. So many times, I have been blamed for his work. But we go well together, Death and Winter, Winter and Death.

Together we dance to the park.

Maria trembles against the pain, biting her lip. Brown hands clench the handrails in the park's single bathroom stall.

She screams as her body rips. She rests for a moment, panting. Despite the cold in the deserted restroom, sweat glistens on her brow and trickles down her cheek. She feels the thrust of a wave of pain and screams again as with a gush of water and blood come relief.

Maria looks down between her legs and sees the profile of a slightly humanoid face. The need to bear down consumes her and Maria finds a sweet release as the little body slithers into toilet bowl. She moves slowly, reaching down to lift the baby as it begins to squirm and whimper in the cold water. She holds it close, sobbing, closing her eyes to the black garbage bag waiting beside her purse.

"I'm sorry. I am so, so sorry."

The park is a magical place on the first snow of winter. Frozen grass sticks up like frosted popsicles leftover from summer. Spears of ice cling to naked branches. Reeds near the lake crash and clatter as I pirouette amongst them. I tickle a sharp-eyed owl to see it shiver.

Death stops.

His head turns towards the pretty little hut.

"Oh yes, it definitely needs Winter's touch." I swirl snow artistically on the shingles. I deck the gutter spout with icicles. The door opens for a young girl and I giggle as I

decorate her with a flurry of snowflakes.
Death stands silently, watching.

"I can't. I can't. I just can't." Maria stumbles from the restroom and braces her back against the door, her breathing sharp and shallow. After a moment she turns back to the sound of the baby's cries. She takes a blue blanket swirled with greens from her purse. She wraps the child tightly and tucks it into her coat. Face set she turns back into the dancing snow.

I watch as the child with a baby stumbles towards the lake and the giant oak with the owl. A trail of blood follows her, sizzling and steaming in the fresh snow, marring its pure beauty. I wave my hand and it is covered.
Death paces alongside the girl, the ends of his cloak caressing her heels.

Maria leans against the tree. She peeps at the precious face in her arms, and then adjusts the blanket. Taking off her coat she makes a nest in the knobby roots of the ancient tree and gently lays the baby down. She pulls the sides together and zips it.

The baby disappears.

Headlights flash as a car turns and crunches into the parking lot. Maria stumbles towards it.

A boy gets out and demands. "Is it done?"

Maria falls onto him sobbing. "I couldn't, Gabe, I just

couldn't. I put him under the tree. It's a boy, Gabe, a beautiful baby boy."

A crack sounds across the park as his fist splits her cheek. She crumples to the snow.

"I told you I didn't want to know. I told you, Maria. Where is it?"

She lifts a shaking hand and points towards the lake. Gabe nods his head once then looks down at the girl. His face changes and he kneels down to help her rise. He holds her tightly, burying his face into her snow sparkled hair.

"I'm sorry. I'm so sorry. It's the only way, Maria. We can't. . ." His anguished voice cracks and stops.

"I know."

"My God, Maria, you're covered in blood."

Maria looks down at her feet, the puddle around her slowly spreading. "I know. It's normal. I think, but I don't know. There was so much blood. There was blood everywhere." Her voice is vague and fading.

Gabe bundles Maria into the car and runs to the restroom to get her things. His large car fishtails out of the park.

I realize that I am alone.

Death rides with the girl in the car.

Curious I walk to the tree, absently laying down fresh snow. The baby's cry reaches me clearly. He is strong where the girl was weak.

But Death has left him. . . for now.

I laugh and the falling snow pulses. I will play a trick on him, my old friend Death. The baby will not die, not tonight.

I look around.

A dog snuffles around a jungle gym on the other side of the park.

I dash towards it. "Come," I breathe, ruffling its long, white hair. The dog whines and follows the scent of the child I bring to it on the wind. It snuffles at the tree and marks it, then finds the coat and the baby.

The dog tucks itself between the coat and the tree, lending its warmth to the baby. I decorate them all with snowflakes.

"Muki! Muki! Come here boy!" Tara quickly rolls up the window, her eyes scanning the night. "Where is he? It should be easy enough to find a huge, white husky!"

"Don't worry. We'll find him." Kevin drove in silence, carefully negotiating the roads slick with new snow.

"Let's try the park. He loves the park and he knows how to get to it from the house."

"Good idea." Kevin slowly approaches the park's entrance, tapping his brakes before making the left turn. There is no other traffic out on the roads tonight, but just in the half hour since they had left the house looking for Muki the roads have become dangerous.

Suddenly from the right, headlights flash. A car fishtails up the park's single lane road, bald tires tearing at the new snow and slipping on the ice underneath.

Kevin stares at the oncoming car, unable to stop it, unable to get out of the way. The driver sees the other car at the last moment, cranks his wheel hard right, and swerves out of the park.

Its bumper clips the brick entrance instead of Kevin and Tara's car. Tara reaches out and grabs Kevin's hand tightly, her face white and scared.

Her soft voice breaks the silence. "I just saw Death, Kevin."

I chuckle as the car pulls into the park. I knew they would come for the big, beautiful dog with a collar. The dog lifts his face and barks when he hears his name. I come closer to the baby, longing to pull the coat away to see its face, but I dare not, dare not if I am to cheat Death of his prey tonight.

"Muki, here boy, come on, boy. Kevin, it's Muki, I hear him. Why won't he come?"

"He might be stuck, caught on something. Get your mittens and hat and let's go." In no time they are sliding towards a tree standing alone in the middle of the park, following the slight path of someone who had been here before. They find Muki under the tree, beside a thick, dark coat.

"There you are, boy, find something to keep you warm?" Kevin ruffles the husky's fur as the dog rises to greet him. "Like you need it, boyo. What's the matter, Tara?"

"Kevin, there's something in the coat. I think it's a baby." Tara kneels quickly, ripping off her mittens as her fingers fumble with the frozen zipper. "I can't get it open." Muki whines as his master kneels to help. The zipper moves too slowly. A muffled cry comes from the coat.

"Never mind, Kevin, help me slip it out this way." Tara reaches up through the bottom of the coat while Kevin holds it open. She fumbles for the bundle inside. Gently she reaches in further, hands pushing aside blanket and coat until she grasps the small, wriggling body and pulls it towards her.

"My God, Tara, it IS a baby."

"It's a newborn, still wet and bloody." Their eyes meet.

"The car!" They say in unison.

"Come on, wrap him up, let's get him to the hospital. Come on, Muki, good boy, good, good boy."

I laugh and spin as the couple hurries to the car. Snow devils dance with me in the sky. Winter and Death may come together to the park, but together they don't always leave.

A Gargoyle's Got To Do...

First Place, Rose City Tyler Comic Con Short Story Contest, 2015

A GARGOYLE'S GOT TO DO, what a gargoyle's got to do. That was mine long before some copycat human decided to get smart and change it. All through the centuries I held true to it, doing my job of protecting the selfish mortals as they exercised both their stupidity and free will. Tonight, was no exception.

I clicked the safety off the crossbow, ran my finger along the bevel of the custom forged broad-head, grinning at the gray blood beading on my finger. Diamond tipped, dipped in silver, edged with salt. Plenty to kill any black-hearted supernatural.

Even me.

The scent of the city rose on the wind. Sickly. Sweet. A fruit past its prime, rotting, just ready for the lightest touch to slough off its skin and show the true depth of the interior disease.

I shook my head to clear my nostrils.

It became more difficult to protect my hometown and follow the two directives given by my creator. Protect Adam's spawn from themselves by killing the supernaturals who thought them fair prey. And NEVER kill a human. No matter how evil, how depraved, *their* lives were sacrosanct.

Problem?

Few humans remained untouched by the darkness anymore, throwing themselves with wild abandon into the abyss. Many times, I would rather just see them burn. They got to make their mistakes and still have a chance at redemption. I, on the other hand, faced the penalty of turning to stone, never to be freed by the moonlight to walk at night.

A living death.

Eyes burned into my back. I ignored the itch. Valora, our oldest sibling, watched from the pinnacle of Saint Micheal's Cathedral of God's Enduring Grace. Centuries ago she became the first to reject the "gift".

Look what a mess the rest of the seven virtues made of the favor anyway. Created in love, we'd become killers for an unworthy race. Four found the easy route, falling in battle— and I couldn't help my jealousy.

So be it.

Tonight, we protected a human who chose the wrong crowd, a coven of vampires to be exact. Claramond had run into them the night before last, but they'd been prepared for her. Tonight, we came for revenge—Oh, and the human.

Below, my bait, my partner, and the last of my family to walk in the flesh, looked up. I tightened my grip on the bow and the resolve in my heart as the scar on her cheek gleamed in the street light's razor glow.

No one marks my sister and lives.

Tonight the knife wielding vamp was in the group scheduled to make an appearance any moment.

"Try to look alluring." I growled, a whisper from a roof two buildings away.

She heard. She leaned back against the cold brick of the alley wall, eying the tavern across the street. The sign, an ogre gripping a dead unicorn and a tankard, swayed in the curly breeze. She arranged her top with a rustle, letting the shoulder of the green halter top slip.

I glanced at the moon. Blood red shrouded in cloud. An ill omen? If one believed such nonsense. I'm a gargoyle. Stone, silver, salt—that's my religion.

"Do you ever regret?" Her voice threaded through the stench like a needle.

My answer was quick. "No."

How could I? Why would I?

The decision to *not regret* was the only freedom I had.

Humans had the clear-cut knowledge of heaven and hell. But gargoyles had no such assurance. I tried not to think of what came after. Sister after sister I carried to the top of the cathedral where they stood for years, faces blurred by time.

No one but me and Claramond remembering their sacrifice.

My response wasn't what she wanted to hear. Even from this distance, I saw her chin harden to stone. "I mean Valora. The others. Giving everything for this race. Regret not having the free will like the humans, being forced to defend them when there is no one worth defending anymore." She snorted. "Even the children are bad. Turn your back and the older ones will slit your throat."

I shrugged. "It is what it is."

I would not question the directive of our creator, not in front of Clari. I suspected long ago we were not to have lasted long enough to see the seven virtues disappear from the human race. To watch them spiral into darkness. We had been abandoned with few directions and it chaffed.

"I know, but sometimes I wish I was as brave as Valora, giving my heart for love."

I snorted. Valora, the humble. Worshiped for her selflessness, bravery. She was the most cowardly of us all. When faced with a lifetime of servitude, she chose the easy way out.

We fought. We died. She watched. I kept my words to myself. Clari's thoughts traveled the same dangerous paths as my own. I did my job. As thankless and as messy as it was—it was our lot.

Through the ages I had defended and looked after her, the baby. So quick to fall in love. So pained when we killed. Even the minataurs got her pity. I sensed her pulling away from this, rethinking.

She thought too much.

Her head turned toward the bar. "He's coming."

I trusted her. With her bleeding heart, she sensed individual people and others. Claramond. Love. I tightened my grip.

"Justine?"

"Yeah."

"However, this turns out, I love you."

A coldness washed over my skin. Before I could ask what she meant, the door opened, revealing our prey.

The human walked at the head of a company of vamps, a giant bringing up the rear. A skinny thing, balding even though he couldn't be more than thirty. Not exactly a vampire prize, even for a late-night snack. The blade of a knife at his hip glowed crimson in the light from the dirty window.

Another omen? Not if I could help it.

I sighted the bolt straight at the cold heart of the monster to his left, easing my finger onto the trigger. A deep breath. I just needed Sis to call out to give me a clear shot.

"Hey there, boys." Fool girl stepped into my line of

fire instead of waiting. What was she trying to do? Get herself killed?

The man stopped as though jerked by a grappling hook. The vamps turned in one motion, like a vee of swans coming in for a landing. If swans had fangs and a blood thirst that is.

But even the undead couldn't deny the virtue of love. Sculpted for passion, her voice seduced, hips, shoulder, neck about which songs had been written. I squelched the green monster wriggling in my heart. I was Justice. And justice would be done.

A vamp put a hand on his shoulder in warning. "Master."

My heartbeat kicked up a notch. Few vamps deigned to call a lower species lord. They considered themselves the princes of darkness. Blood-sucking egomaniacs more like it.

The man shrugged the hand off with a disregard I had never seen a descendant of Adam demonstrate to a supernatural. Warning bells clanged in my gut.

He approached my sister with every confidence of a lover, noses nearly touching. "Clari would never hurt me. Would you now?" The human lifted his hand, his thumb traced the scar. My rage erupted. I pulled the trigger.

The kiss of the blade cutting the thick air was enough. The vamp trying to stop lover boy leaped forward, using his own body to block the bolt. It sank home, a satisfying thump of metal in flesh. But he did not disintegrate as he should have.

Pandemonium broke.

The vamps tightened around their prize, blocking my sibling from view. I leaped down the four stories to give them a target.

Snarling, the wounded vamp tore the bolt from the flesh of his shoulder. Obviously not a vamp. *My bad.*

He pointed at me. "Take it."

That made me laugh. *As if.*

I ran to meet them. Seven against one. Not too bad. I'd fought against worse odds. But all the other times I had a sister at the very least by my side. We could take anything together, but I was alone. Clari behind the line. Our own ranks grew dangerously thin.

I didn't bother ducking the blows of the vamps. Like spring rain on granite, they rolled off my skin. I jerked a bolt from the quiver at my side and stuck it in the nearest. He burned to ash and smoke, releasing the weapon so I could turn it on another and another.

Three down.

I kept my eye on the giant. He might be a problem. Another fanged menace tried to bite me. I laughed at the sound of the tooth tinkling on the cobblestones of the alley.

"Fool." Too bad for him he never faced a gargoyle before. I slammed the bolt into his neck and turned to roll under the swipe of the giant's club. The swing broke the neck of one of his little vamp friends. The blow wouldn't kill the beast, but it gave me a minute to reassess.

Four ash. One out. This left me, one undamaged vamp, and the giant. The blood sucker's eyes darted around. He didn't like these odds at all. That split second of hesitation proved his undoing. I grabbed his hand and jabbed. Smoke and ash.

I motioned to the giant. "Just you and me now, blockhead." I dropped the bolt. No good against his rock-like skin.

I flicked my eyes to Clari. Bossy vamp looking creature leaned against the building as though bored, black eyes pinned on me, calling. I nearly got my head taken off as the giant attacked. I rolled past the oaf, palming my own diamond knife and slicing at the Achilles.

I turned, victorious, just in time to see Clari drive a knife into Adam's spawn.

"No!" The scream ripped from my lips and I ran to her. Grey seeped up her outstretched hand, the fingers freezing.

"I'm sorry, Justine. I just couldn't do it anymore. All the killing." Claramond. Love. What kind of sick monster made the virtues into the things they chased? I could handle it, but each kill pulled her closer to this madness. "Shall I pose into something inspiring? Like Valora?"

We both looked. Big Sis stood with an arm upraised holding a sword above the city as though daring evil to make its home here. Too late for that. I longed to curl up and cry like an orphaned bat.

The virtue of love pulled herself straight. "I wish I wore a dress." The words were muffled, her lips ashing before my eyes.

"You would."

And then she was stone and those were my last words to her. I wondered at the coldness creeping over my body. My limbs feeling like they did at the turning, sluggish. I should have told her I loved her. But what good would it do? She left me alone.

"Wow. You don't see that every day."

Except for the bossy thing who didn't have the manners to die when I shot him. I growled and whirled, throwing my blade from my hip at the same time. He ghosted aside, right into the second knife.

It thunked into his chest just where it should, shredding flesh and the very human-like heart underneath.

He eyed the rose of blood budding on his shirt. "Interesting."

I waited for it. The guy wasn't a supernatural, humanoid race—maybe an elf. Close enough. Elves and dwarfs were part of the no kill clause. His death would release me. He'd probably made a deal with the devil to be hanging out with this group.

I ruminated over my regrets. Not many really. As the virtue of Justice, I delighted sending evil back to the abyss. Monsters did get their just deserts in the end. I wiggled my foot. Still flesh, damp in its boot.

The elf wheezed and dropped to the ground. Maybe it didn't work because he wasn't dead yet. A problem easy enough to remedy. I stalked towards him, just in time to see his eyes glaze.

Now the end could come. I knew I didn't have time to get me and Clari back to the cathedral and our perches near our sisters where we belonged, but it would have been nice. I wiggled my fingers, the first to change on my sweet sibling.

Nothing.

"What's going on?" I demanded of the rats scuffling in the dumpster.

"Justice."

I turned at the voice. A shimmering figure about the size of a small dwarf lighted the blood-stained bricks.

Great. An Angel. Insufferable snobs. This was the last thing I needed on a truly horrible night.

"What do you want, lamp stick."

The glow faded. "Be nice, Gar-girl."

"Go away." I closed my eyes, trying to encourage the turning. Nothing.

"That's not going to work."

"Why are you still here? Go away."

"You asked for answers. I pulled the pin feather. It's justice. You don't get to turn. You're the last. All of you turned traitor to your kind. Just look at this mess. Couldn't follow a few simple rules—Don't kill the sons and daughters of

Adam."

"Look who's talking. You lost a third of your crew to rebellion *and* caused The Fall."

The angel winced, but at least he doused the glow and quit the hovering thing. It settled on the ground and I could see how it really appeared. The description of the angels in Revelation had nothing on this one. All four faces were that special kind of spectre that even gave supernaturals nightmares. This was the terrible kind of angel, the one that used mummies to kill the first born of Egypt.

Angels got to do all the fun things.

"So, then. You will continue on, defend and protect the humans."

I raised my chin. "No." Why would I keep doing it? I had no reason to live. My sisters all stone. That is what I wanted.

"What?"

"I won't do it."

"You can't say no."

"I just did. And there's no way some winged midget is going to tell me otherwise." I waited for it. The bolt of lightening to reprimand me for sassing the Big Guy's messenger.

Nothing.

Except the midget in question did the head spinning thing and I got a look at a whole new visage. Eww. I stepped forward and drove my last dagger into its neck.

"I. Said. No."

A flash and a screech then the nightmarish messenger disappeared, leaving me alone among the dead bodies and one statue. Guess I won't turn until dawn. But there were other ways for a gargoyle to die. I just had to figure one out. I threw my little sister over my shoulder and started towards St. Mike's.

A gargoyle's got to do what a gargoyle's got to do.

Right?

Scion of Captain Hook

Honorable mention, NETWO Short Short Contest, 2019

THE FAIRY WAS CARELESS.

Good. It made the hunt that much easier.

Pixie dust scattered on the game trail she followed glinted in the weak moonlight threading through the firs. It lifted Hana's feet until she hovered inches off the ground, allowing her to move that much more silently. She bent the ferns aside with painstaking care and let them fall closed with a sound softer than a whisper.

Laughter tinkled like the falling of icicles only two or three trees ahead. Pressing her body flat against the ground and using the charmed dust to scoot bare centimeters above the thick carpet of needles, Hana caught a glimpse of her quarry.

Think happy thoughts, she reminded herself, *happy*

thoughts, happy thoughts. With this catch I will finally prove I am the greatest of all fairy hunters. She ignored the cavorting of her stomach at the thought. *Just get it over with.*

The fairy she sought danced with several of her kind in jasmine scented glade. Ivory pale with enormous blue eyes, and golden hair tied in a bun wreathed with yarrow, lavender, and honey suckle, she flitted under the full Hunter's moon. A human child slept at the center of the cavorting fairy, oblivious to the enchantment lulling it to sleep.

Hana shook her head. Foolish fairies would never learn. Humans just did not like their children disappearing. Not even when replaced with a fairy child or given a fae gift—the gift of beauty especially tended to be a curse more than a boon. Hana felt her own face, the ridged scar lines, the half-closed lid of a milk white eye. That wasn't even the worst of it. One of the arms bending back the foliage screen ended in a wicked hook.

With a silent oomph, Hana dropped to the ground.

Happy thoughts. Happy thoughts.

I will finally fit in with the Hooks once and for all.

It wasn't particularity easy to stand out in a family of extraordinary fairy hunters. Pixie dust, the golden glitter shed by the smallest of the spritely folk was a valuable commodity. Just a few feel good thoughts and one could take to the air like the nimblest swallow.

Though Hana's family founder, a nasty pirate by the name of Captain Hook, met a terrible end in the jaws of an alligator with a clock fetish, the rest of the family excelled at bagging and selling sprites. The wee ones didn't do well in captivity, fading to shades within a few weeks, so the market remained lucrative. Of course, fairies weren't all light joy, especially when angry, and fought back when they could. Thus, the horrific countenances of most fairy hunters. Including Hana's.

Her thoughts refused to supply the levity needed to levitate, so Hana remained on her belly, damp seeping through her clothes, watching the fairy which had led her family on a chase for generations. If only she could catch the evil thing, no one would laugh at her. They might hide their faces and cringe away, but no one would laugh.

Her palm caught a vibration tunneling through the ground with the steady rhythm of footsteps. *Hunters!*

And clumsy ones at that. She pressed her ear to the ground. She calculated the others to be at least a mile off, but closing fast, most likely led by a trained badger. Maybe even a fox. *Poachers,* she snarled inwardly.

This was Hana's hunt. She would bring this fairy in and claim the fame for the Hook family name. Her thoughts brought her above the ground again, so she pulled her net gun from her belt and checked the load. She jiggled the bark spiders in the see-through canister to set them to work, licked a finger and held it up. This low breeze would not be a factor, but she would have to stand to get the proper arc for the net. And get closer. She inched around the perimeter of the glade, taking her time, blocking out the approach of the other hunters. The fairy in the leafy skirt and petal bodice dancing without a single care consumed Hana's entire attention.

Finally, Hana gathered her legs under her, taking an extra pinch of pixie dust from her own pouch and casting it over her body. Several successful hunts showed that most fairies scattered to their right. Hana planned to shoot up and over the dance, firing down and to the fairy's principal side.

The fairies fluttered to a stand still, drifting above the child but staring off towards the ocean. The child, a boy older than Hana first thought and dressed all in green with a cocky red feather in an archer's hat, woke and sat up.

Not a human child. Not just a boy. It was the original Lost Boy. The one that refused to grow up, even when given every chance. Even after rescue mission after rescue mission sought out his most secret places. Peter Pan.

He yawned and stretched as though he had not a care in the world then cocked his head towards the sound of pursuit. With a chortle he leaped to his feet and bounded into the air.

"We'll give these hunters a merry chase," he cried. Drawing his short sword, he crowed loudly, following it with a wild laugh. He pointed down at the largest fairy. "Wait here, Tink, and play bait while I lay the traps."

The fairy's merry laughter joined his own and she waved as the boy and the other fairies disappeared into the trees.

Hana didn't hesitate. It didn't get any better than this.

She leaped into the air, somersaulting into position. The joy of the hunt gave impetuous to those elusive happy thoughts. She fired the net gun on the roll. Enormous blue eyes followed her, the Fairy's bell like chimes of fading laughter changing to the clanging gongs of fear. She darted right. The net fell. By the time Hana completed her arc, the fairy fell to the ground tangled in the reinforced spider web.

"Yes," Hana crowed in a voice to match the wild boy's. She rushed to her prize, pulling out the iron fairy cage. The sprite cringed back, tremendous tears welling in her eyes.

Hana whipped the web from the sprite and had her in the cage in two quick breaths. The fairy whispered, the bells reaching a high pitch of pleading.

Hana shook the cage. "None of that, Tinker Bell. I have heard of your games and I know them all," she snorted. "No Hook is going to fall for that innocent little fairy routine."

If possible, the fairy's countenance grew even more fearful. Hana chuckled, though pain at the fairy's fear gnawed at her stomach. "That's right. I'm a Hook. Now you know and I will finally bring victory to our family." She held the cage up, admiring her prize.

Tink grabbed the bars of her prison and reached out with a hand, pleading, pointing towards the way the Lost Boy had disappeared.

"Nope. You're mine. Not his any more." The words

echoed hollowly. Hadn't her ancestor said those very words when he used Tink as bait for Peter? She shrugged. It didn't matter. "Time to get you weighed and tagged."

A shout pulled her attention to the woods and she clutched the cage close. She knew that voice! "Hugo!" she hissed.

Her brother and bane of of her existence must lead the other hunters. No way would she allow him to steal this one from her. She stepped out of the glen as another voice yelled out, this time in pain.

"Seems like your boy has been busy," she observed to her captive.

The fairy's eyes grew bright and she covered her mouth to smother a wicked laugh, but she pointed at Hana.

Hana couldn't help her own grin. "You think I will fall for The Boy's traps? I don't think so. I actually listened when Grandpa Hook told us those stories. I know all of Peter's tricks."

Hana covered the cage with a black cloth, effectively dousing the fairy light. About five feet into the woods, she took a pinch of the extra dust and tossed it into the air.

This time flying came easily and she rose to the top of a fir towering above all the others. From this height she could see the green flash of Peter followed by his fairy friends. They circled a darker, heavier group closer to the ground—her brother no doubt. She opened the cover just a crack so Tink could enjoy the show.

This would be fun.

Peter would give her brother a good kick in the pride and Hana would return with the prize. She settled into watch. She wouldn't miss this for the world. Just as she thought Peter had the hunter though, all the lights flashed out and the Lost Boy tumbled to the ground. Hugo's hunters shouted in triumph.

Both Tink and Hana leaned forward.

"No," Hana murmured. They caught the Lost Boy. This couldn't be happening. Just when she thought victory within her grasp.

Peter's form struggled and kicked, but he was just a boy. Hugo's hunters were grown men, hardened by the hunt and merciless. The fairy light in the cage dimmed, reflecting Hana's mood. Despite the fact she herself was a hunter, she wanted to cry.

A diminutive hand touched her finger.

Hana dashed the traitorous wetness from her face. "What?"

"Hook," Tink chimed, pointing towards the victorious hunter.

"Yeah. That's a Hook too and it looks like he's going to win this round." Along with how many other rounds? Hugo cheated and lied—anything to get the dust. She leaned her forehead on the cage. And all Hana had was the fairy.

The little hand touched the bow of her lip where a scar twisted her mouth into a perpetual grimace. Hana jerked back, but a tiny ball of warm traveled from her lips, across her cheek, down her throat to settle just above her heart.

"You're no Hook," Tink chimed.

Hana looked away from the earnest gaze. "I *am* a Hook." She lifted the arm missing a hand. "See?"

Tink pointed at the warm spot on her chest. "Not here. Not where it counts," chimed the Fairy's bells.

She knew. How could she know Hana's failures? That though she successfully captured fairies, she turned very few in. She hated to see their beautiful lights fade to gray. Wild faces dimmed with sadness. Sure, she loved the feel of pixie dust—who didn't? But she hated where it came from. She hated that she had to be a part of it. This was the true reason the Hook family ostracized her. She was a terrible hunter.

Hana took off the black cloth and opened the door. "You're right. Go save your boy." Tink could, and would, do it. She had done it so many times over the years when Peter got himself into trouble. Tink executed a double somersault in the air and zipped away.

Pixie dust and happy thoughts expended, Hana drifted slowly to the ground. "Yeah, I'm a terrible Hook anyway. Always will be."

Something zinged her shoulder and she whirled. A light dove at her face again and then stilled. Tink hovered just inches away, face wreathed with smiles.

She held a vial out to Hana. "Drink," chimed the Fairy. "Be free."

Hana took the glass between her thumb and forefinger, afraid of crushing the gift.

"From the King," said Tink.

"Fairy gifts," Hana groused.

But Tink disappeared in a wink. Hana opened the vial. The scent of green and blue filled her senses, rain and moss.

"Be free," she repeated. A dream flitted at the edges of her consciousness. One where she was anything but a Hook .

"To freedom." Before she could think, she tossed the bit of liquid to the back of her throat.

Pain ripped through every cell, lightning leaked from every pore. She screamed, scuttling back against the trunk of the fir, pressing her back into the rough bark. It could not hold her. She dropped to the ground and writhed forever.

★★★★★★★

"Miss, Miss, wake up."

Hana opened her eyes and stared into the scarred face of her brother. "Hugo?"

Her brother stepped back, expression startled. "You know me?" he demanded.

Hana reached back for the tree to help her stand, no sense asking her brother for help., she snapped, "of course I know you, you're my—"

Instead of the unbalanced feel of hand and hook on the truck, fingers from *both* hands felt the sturdy column. She held her arms out, gazing at two perfect hands with long fingers and crescent nails. She touched her face, tracing the perfect bow of her lips, the smooth curve of the cheek that should still bear the scars of salamander fire.

"Bewitched," muttered one of the men behind her brother.

Hugo nodded. "Good thing we came upon you, Miss, the fairies were no doubt planning to steal you away. But you said you knew me, I would remember someone as beautiful as you, I'm sure." He leered down at her.

Hana shook her head. "No, never mind. I was mistaken. I don't know you." She straightened, finding herself taller, her body changed. The men gawked at her. She looked down at her hunting clothes, decidedly too small and clinging to a woman's curves she had not possessed before drinking the Tink's potion.

"I don't know any of you." she said and followed the path deeper into the forest.

Free from the Hook legacy at last.

C.I. Chevron

Freedom Fighter

"**Freeze! Code 30. Officer 7287** requesting backup at a 10-54. Possible 187. Pacifier present, but–uh–I think he's the perp. Can they do things like that?"

"Copy, Officer 7287. Stand-by."

Crouching over the body, the monster ignored the words behind his right shoulder. Carefully he lifted the girl. Her torso fit the length of his bicep and her legs, no wider than three of his blunt fingers, draped across his thigh. Her head lolled. Eyes, so empty not minutes before, stared up at him, forgiveness a lingering light in the softness of her expression.

Life, still seeping from the broken form, melted away like smog before a persistent breeze. He cradled her close, smoothed walnut colored strands. A finger traced the single fist size bruise around the delicate throat.

He slid his palm around once more until it fit perfectly. "Be free."

No other mark marred the creamy perfection of a body modified for pleasure. Only his, the mark of a monster bio-engineered for brute strength in a size meant to intimidate the most defiant protester.

A heavy hand slammed on the meaty muscles of his shoulder. "I said freeze."

He raised his eyes to the black armored Enforcer. A gun trembled three feet away, barrel aimed somewhere between his translucent polycarbonate eyes and carbon fiber nose.

Foolish un-enhanced human didn't have the sense of a Driobe, those pesky, ubiquitous rodents that would die rather than abandon a morsel of food. Only the stupid or insane stepped within the reach of a pacifier.

The officer's mic crackled. "Officers on the way. Do not engage."

The recruit stepped back on stiff legs, evidently realizing his folly, but unwilling to give ground.

The Pacifier turned back to the frail Keisa. Her desperate touch had startled him as he strode through the neighborhood. It brought his integrated comp online to report the coordinates of his stop and with it the awareness of his location. *Home.* She'd asked for so little, freedom. As a Pacifier he could not, would not refuse.

He laid her at his feet, crossing arms over chest, and rose to his full two and a half meters. His gaze traveled over the gray block building shadowing the debris littered street. Eyes pierced him from the shadows–evil eyes, empty eyes, lost eyes—even hopeful eyes. The windows from the first to fourth floor gaped like missing teeth, except for one.

She stood in all her glorious nudity, black eyes pinned to his face. Her sculpted body, a study of feminine perfection, a living billboard for the services within. A shackle, hard iron on a creamy wrist, ensured her continued vigil. It could last for hours, released only when she had a visitor.

The monster stared. Waiting. It came. A movement, imperceptible to human eyes, a defiant lift of arched brow, the tilt of the surgically altered chin.

Released from the shackles of chemical and orders, the Pacifier spread his arms wide and roared, loosing the fire boiling within. No matter what originally brought him to this black street of his past, nothing mattered but her face.

Her will superseded all, beckoning him to action, to finish what he should have years ago, actions only the hopelessness of her current situation could command. Pacifiers did not kill, they pacified. People dying in the process ended up to be merely circumstantial.

The enforcer lunged from the path of the scorching flames, covering his head and eyes with fowl-like squawks.

Ignoring the officer, he turned a three sixty and stalked towards the tenements. He stepped up the curb and his eyes clouded, reliving the past. No longer a mutated monster, he crouched in the street. Gutters gushed with fallen ran, washing them clean of blood and urine for a short time.

Beside him crouched the girl who would become Keisa, not as she was now, pulled by others into shapes of beauty unnatural and to his eyes unbecoming, but just another snot faced girl child reeking of the sins of her parents.

Lily.

She laughed at his paper boats stacked with cigarette butt people rushing down the gushing cataract. He watched until each one disappeared, wishing such liberation could be so easy.

Today, the chained and barred door to his old home blistered and crackled with the first fist fall, shattered into enough kindling to fuel fires for a krono.

Shadows scurried. He ignored them, pacing towards the steps gray with the residue of ruined lives. A crack reverberated in the tight spaces, the sound adding more spiderweb fissures in plaster un-repaired since before the Fall. His shoulder stung once, twice, three times. He paused on the landing.

Foolish boy. He should have learned in Academy Enforcer weapons would never stop a Pacifier in the thrall of *Incendia*. Blood turned his vision crimson.

Tink. Tink. Tink.

The engineered body expelled the projectiles lodged between resilin epidermis and polyethylene silicon carbide hybrid dermis. He pulled himself upward. Filigree railing, as delicate as the body in the street, crumpled beneath his grasp. He passed the first hall and moved on to the second set of stairs.

Memories overwhelmed him once more. He and the girl smoked on the landing. He much bigger, she already under going the arduous torments paid for by her handlers to turn her into something else.

He had not been sold yet.

With the wisdom of a child, he sensed his time grew short. It shrank in the face of the calculating eye of his father judging length of limb and bulge of adolescent muscle, the increasing drunkenness of his mother. He lay his hand on a thigh grimy with the dirt of the street. Her warmth spread through his fingers. She looked at him through eyes swollen with the latest surgery then kissed him with desperate lips.

On the landing he learned what she would be, and what he would never have.

Later, he stepped into the one-bedroom apartment. His mother dangled a baby in one pocked hand. His father sprang from behind and injected sedative into his fragile neck.

Time had run out.

Even now the pain of betrayal, no matter how long he'd known it would happen, allowed the napalm to slip past his control. He opened his mouth and breathed out the agony, coating the walls of the second floor with flame. It flickered then crept up the wall, devouring paint and paper. He stepped through to the first door on the left.

It crumpled before the weight of his shoulder like crepe paper. Two strangers struggled to their feet, drug fogged eyes squinting then widening as it seemed to sink into befuddled brains that a Pacifier stood in their door.

"Hello, Mom. Dad." His voice grated like razors over glass. Even an armored throat could only take so much abuse and still produce sound.

He'd heard that newer models drank a special coating to make it easier. But for those like him, bartered for the price of a girl child destined to supply parental retirement income, got the bare bones enhancements. Dependent, of course, on the buyer.

The woman screamed, drawing his attention to the task for which he'd come, one programmed into him by abuse and neglect long before the lab got a hold of him.

She threw a pillow with one hand, clutched the bottle of booze in the other. More objects hurled his way, but the sly side step of his father brought him around.

"Welcome home–" Crafty eyes scanned his bare forearms for his call sign. "Titan." The old man approached as though to hug the beast. As though smoke did not roil in the hall, as though his door did not litter the floor.

The embers in his gut ignited to an inferno, struggled to be released. He sighed, a gust of fire coating man and woman with flames. They jerked and danced and screamed like marionettes at a street fair. The couch ignited. A lamp fell, starting a conflagration of its own. Booze spilled and burned blue.

Still they shrieked. The different pitches combining into a melody that rose and fell, it crescendoed, beating on his ears like the wings of a Sontha Bird flitting from flower to flower. He'd seen them in the gardens of his employer while he watched a girl child in a white dress play. She would never be sold.

She had him.

"Mommy?" A child stood in the doorway of the second room, red hair tousled from sleep, eyes wide as they took in the hellish play that decimated her home. The wailing died to low moans then only the crackle pop of the flames growing broke the silence.

Two smoking figures lay twisted and blackened where they'd fallen.

Titan tried to turn away, retreat the way he had come, escape. But her eyes rose to his, met and held. In them no monster stared back.

Sister.

He strode through the flames, clothes smoking, skin impervious. She leaped at him before he made it halfway across the room, as though her tiny soul recognized and gravitated to his strength. For the second time that night he held softness close to his heart.

He whirled. The police officer blocked his way, gun braced, coughing smoke from his lungs. "Stop there!"

Persistent bugger.

A man that stupid did not deserve to live.

Titan shifted the girl to the arm away from the threat, then sprang forward and crushed the man's skull with a hammer fist. He knelt briefly, reloading the gun and jamming extra clips into multiple pant pockets.

He strode down the stairs to the basement, the girl riding secure on his hip. He set her down for only a moment as he ripped the gas line from the wall, then made his way to the first floor once again. He stood in the doorway.

Watching, waiting.

They came, slowly at first, those eyes from the darkness, materializing into people. Beautiful girls, hags long spent, men without limbs, monsters like him, chemicals needed to produce *Incendia* spent, minds gone from war or drugs.

They crowded around him, caressing the gun in his hand with reverent fingers.

He looked up. Lily stared back, eyes sharp with anticipation–longing. Her chained arm rose, fingers pressed on the glass separating them.

She remembers. A death pact made in the mocking seriousness of children, one pushed from his memory until now.

Hands took control of his, guiding the banned weapon to a wrinkled brow. He did not look down. His finger, almost too large for the trigger guard, squeezed the tiny mechanism.

With a soft sigh another soul flew free. Another and another fell—any who asked. He fired until the the gun glowed red, then he reloaded and continued.

Finally, with empty pockets and the human shaped shells piled at his feet, he dropped the weapon and raised his gaze to hers. Would *she* call him monster?

She smiled.

The fire boiled in his gut. He breathed deep. The bitter scent of fuel filled his nostrils.

He roared for the last time, pulling every bit *Incendia* napalm from his cells, enough to level a squalid city block.

Grime Partners Cleaning Service

THE CLEANING BUSINESS CAN BE PRETTY TAME. I don't mean the type of cleaning where you solve problems with a gun. No, the cleaning that takes place after the type of cleaner that employs a gun.

I, however, have a specialty type of cleaning business, one that cleans up after a crime. No one wants to come home to brains and blood, so besides toilets, which I do very well and can make shine like a model's caps, I know all every little trick to remove body fluids from a variety of surfaces.

Tuesday's e-mail, however, hinted at a cleaning that sounded a little off. Seeing that the message supplied an address, and me being the suspicious person that I am, I Googled it.

Sure enough, the first thing that came across was a hit in the local Daily Tribune. Four charred remains found in Highland Oaks area.

Hmmmm. Tricky.

I emailed back pretty quickly. Things like that don't scare me off, I wouldn't be in this business if it did, but charred remains usually meant smoke smell throughout the house, damage to the flooring or nearby furniture. Things difficult to get completely resolved.

I asked the usual—the big thing being price–and voiced my concerns. Shoving aside a a host of red marked hospital bills to get to my keyboard.

Symthrin@skyweb.com: I have studied your website and understand your concerns. I will pay $2000 for two hours of your time and $100 for every hour after that.

My jaw dropped and that suspicious nature of mine flared.

Not that I didn't need the money, who didn't, but crime scene clean up didn't pay that well.

"What's the catch?" My fingers flew across the keyboard, asking Mr. Symthrin the same question. Symthrin? Sounded like a drug to me. Maybe he's a dealer.

"No catch. I simply require your time and am willing to pay."

"Well, then I'm willing to work." I muttered as I answered to that respect, but in a more professional tone, of course.

★★★

The next day, I rang the antique doorbell surrounded by teeth.

"Ouch!" I sucked at the blood welling in a pinprick. I leaned closer.

A small needle of light, as though sensing my presence, withdrew like an eel. I twisted my neck to look up at a gargoyle embedded in the stone above the door. "Very funny."

Sheesh, when are people going to learn somethings just aren't funny. Probably about the time they learn large doesn't necessarily equate with classy. And sick jokes are always sick.

I sighed as I looked over the Gothic structure, all twisted spires. On the drive up, I'd counted four chimneys rising above the tiled roof. Who the hell needed four fireplaces?

I tapped my foot, no answer. Checked my phone to make sure I had the right day, and for the hundredth time that morning wished my sister and my best friend, stood beside me.

Grime Partners Cleaning Service is small, just my twin, Hyali, and me. Rule number one of the business, never go anywhere alone.

Like I could help it.

My sister's constant complaining of constipation had actually been a tumor. Tomorrow she would go under the knife to get it removed, along with a section of her large intestine that would mean a colostomy for the rest of her life.

Besides all that, the bills, and now the hospital, still needed paid.

So here I stood.

Alone.

I made sure the needle stayed retracted and rang the bell again. Gongs that I hadn't heard before sounded from somewhere far away.

Second time's a charm, I guess.

The door swung open without any help. I bit back another sigh. The whole creepy vibe had been done. Besides, I'd seen worse in far more frightening places.

I lugged my Kirby over the threshold and into a foyer the size of my apartment.

Dark paneled walls reached up three stories. A black marble staircase the width of the length of my VW winded away up out of sight.

Yep, perfect place for a quadruple homicide by burning. I sniffed.

No odor.

"Hello?" I shut the door and immediately began to snoop. The first door on the right—locked. Second, locked.

Left, same thing.

"Hello. Grime Partners Cleaning Service."

Yes, my last name is Grime.

"Upstairs, please."

I squelched a little jump of my heart and glared around for an intercom. He thought speaking through some hidden device would scare me. In reality it ticked me off.

At twenty-six I'd cleaned a lot of houses. My sister and I started doing this six years ago and added crime scenes once we got some good referrals.

Maybe it didn't classify as a dream job, but when you're kicked out of a foster home at seventeen, there are very few open opportunities that don't require a huge expenditure outright. School being one of them. It beat flipping burgers and paid better besides.

I stopped on the landing to catch my breath. Cleaning kept me in shape, but the older type Kirby vacuums are beasts and *heavy.* I stared back at the rest of my equipment and frowned. Better find the room first.

As though reading my mind, the disembodied voice spoke again. "Please continue."

Yeash, the place had to have wires everywhere to get that sort of surround sound.

With a grunt, I headed for the third floor. Near the top step, the acrid scent of burned hair singed my nostrils. The slightly burnt smell of flesh, as though someone left the steak on the grill too long.

I followed my nose down the wide hall with a window at the end, to the only open door—second on the right—the one with the crime scene tape.

"Hello?" Not really expecting anyone to answer, I rolled the yellow and black length into a ball and stepped over the threshold.

"Please come in."

"Okay. You can stop with the creepy voice now. I'm here, I know it's a crime scene. I can do my job just as well, better even, without theatrics."

"Indeed."

I stepped around the couch. More crime tape. Strangest tape job I've ever seen. This time surrounding four substantial piles of ash. Odd that there had been no tape or evidence of police activity on the outside. My senses started tingling.

Walking quickly to the floor length window and tired of the whole vampire vibe the Gothic mansion, not the mention the owner, threw off, I jerked them open.

I grinned to myself and turned, expecting to see my mysterious somewhat odd employer smoking on the Persian carpet.

The room remained empty. Well, of life anyway.

Bright sunlight from a cool fall day now flooded the room, illuminating every corner from a knock off Venus statue in one to a potentially authentic Ming vase in another. A cavernous fireplace took a whole wall between the two. I figured I could stand in it, and was tempted to try, but duty called. Besides, it might be tasteless in a room with people who'd been crispy crittered.

"That was rude."

The voice floated from everywhere and no where. It bounced around in my head as though it were my sister's, or my conscience, and I began to suspect I imagined it.

Just a game I'd set up to entertain myself and make up for the absence of my sister. She, at least, would be wisecracking right along with me. In fact, I'd probably be hauling her out of the fire pit.

I unwound the vacuum cord and looked for an outlet. Time to put these ashes to rest. I wondered why no body wanted them, shouldn't they be buried or something?

Still. My number only came up after everything was said and done, the police must have all they needed. I eyed the ash piles, gauging size. Nothing the Kirby couldn't handle, of course. Good thing I brought extra bags.

"Allow me." The vacuum roared to life. I looked at the plug and then the wall, then the vacuum. Okay, that creeped me out a little.

I stepped on the pedal. The motor quit.

"Okay. Do you want me to clean the ash piles up or not?"

"In time."

"So, what do you want?"

"A moment. I did pay for two hours, did I not?"

I froze, my heart rate kicking up a notch. "Yes. But

this isn't one of those full-service companies, you know. Nothing kinky. I keep all my clothes on, and you stay. . .whereever you are."

You wouldn't believe how many times I'd been propositioned at a crime scene for extra services. Like blood and guts turned people on. I might not get all bent out of shape about it, but yuck.

A chuckle sounded around me. "Nothing kinky then. Why don't you sit?"

"I like standing." The better to get the heck out of here if need be. I reached for the leg pocket of my cleaning scrubs and my phone.

"That will not be necessary. I have agreed to your terms."

"I'd feel better." I started to thumb 911, my finger poised over the green button.

An electrical charge shot up my arm. My phone went black. "Hey!"

Did he do that? I shook the device and poked the on button. Nothing. "What did you do to my phone?" It was the only way Hyali could reach me. I looked around for a land line. Nothing.

Defeated I stepped to the couch and sat. "Fine. What do you want?"

"I need a certain type of service, one not specified by the yellow pages."

"So, you e-mailed me?"

"As a crime scene cleaning company you have a lot of experience with the strange, and, as you have demonstrated already, aren't afraid of much."

I nodded. So far, all true. I motioned to the ash piles. "So, you don't need these cleaned?"

"You seemed preoccupied with the piles."

"Well, they were people."

"Yet you were going to vacuum them?"

I shrugged. "Least they'd be gone. Might even bury them." Not sure where, but it was a good thought.

A chuckle. "That is true. If it relieves your mind some, they were not really people."

"Really?"

"No. They were previous applicants"

Okay, now I'm freaked. "And the police report?"

"Fake."

"Why?"

"I knew you would check. As you may have noticed, electronics of this world come easily to me."

Not sure if I liked how he said 'this world'. This guy had some serious issues.

"Listen. Hate to burst your bubble, but I'm not into role playing games or the whole vampire/zombie scene. If you think you came from another world, that's fine by me, but leave me out of it. Honestly, I just want to do my job."

"This is no game."

I lifted a shoulder. "Okay." No need to make the

sociopath angry. He could be violent. He seemed to catch the drift of my thoughts, so of course, he became angry, and violent.

"This is not a game!" Lights flashed on and off, doors slammed, electricity sizzled spat from those previously unseen outlets.

I sat very still. I turned, the door was shut. Trapped three stories up. I could try and run for it, on the off chance the door wasn't locked, but I hated to leave the Kirby, those things were expensive and that one had been with us since the beginning.

I leaned back. "Okay. What's this service?"

"We need a corporeal body."

I slapped my face and rubbed my eyes. Those sleepless nights at the hospital were catching up with me. "AS I stated, I don't do that."

A sigh wrapped around me. Loneliness and desperation not my own sent goose bumps chasing up my arms. Ice formed on the inside of the windows. I wrapped my arms around me.

Would a fall from a three-story window hurt?

A flame flared in the firebox. "Perhaps we should start over."

"That might be good."

The single voice split into many ranging the scale, all in perfect harmony. Power swelled, shrinking the huge room. "We are Symthrin."

I cleared my throat past the sudden constriction. Fear? No, just my mind having a great conversation with itsself. Denial, such a lovely thing. "Nice to meet you. I'm Harper."

"Delighted."

Well wasn't this just nice.

"I found your cleaning site on the world wide web. You possess a uniqueness we find appealing."

"My type O blood."

"We are not vampires."

"Oh good."

"No. You go from house to house, places filled with great emotion."

"The places I go are crime scenes, not good emotions, messy places." I eyed the pile of ash. "Usually."

"Emotions leave electrical residue long after people have felt them."

I motioned to the piles at my feet. "or have any use of them?"

"Yes."

"So, you just want to hitch around on me?"

"Yes."

I stood. "No."

That over with, I grabbed the handle of my Kirby and headed for the door. I am so not coming to a building alone again. If Hyali and I had to start a new business—so be it. I had a little saved back, in cash so the hospital wouldn't see it. We could move—

"Stay."

I pulled on the handle. The solid door didn't budge. "I said no."

"There is nothing that you need? We are are versatile. It would only be for a few months, then you would be free to go on with your life. Richer perhaps."

"Money doesn't buy happiness." I chanted. Though it did smooth the way, especially after a $100,000 surgery and more expenses looming.

"No, you are right. But you are worried about something, if not finances, health then? A sister?"

"How in the—?"

"It is in your blood, we tasted it at the door."

"Okay, that's just sick."

The voice ignored me. "We can help—smooth things."

Maybe it could read my mind. "Get out of my head."

The room cooled again. "We are not in your head, but the body is electrical, so are we, your thoughts are obvious from here."

I sat silent. Maybe this was a breakdown from loss of sleep and worry. Served me right, jumping at the money and getting pulled into this. Maybe guilt from the anger I held at Hyali for getting sick and abandoning me to do this on my own had turned into a haunting.

But what if it wasn't?

What if this Symthrin could help me? All they wanted

was a right here and there, feeding off the emotions? They could have some of mine. And if it meant a little less worry about where the money would come from. I started to dream, I could see my sister in the best medical facilities, the best doctors and care. The side long glances would be gone. It would all be worth it. A breeze shifted the ashes, drawing my eye. The alternative didn't look very good from here either.

For Hyali then. "Okay."

As though my acquiescence was invitation enough, a shadow moved where I thought there were none. I closed my eyes, maybe I didn't want to see this. I snapped them open. No, I would see what I had done.

Like tentacles, lightening reached out from a small source, a mini fireworks ball. Beautiful indeed, deadly, certainly. I held my breath. What have I done?

Long fingers touched my skin. It didn't zing like expected, my hairs stood up, but that was it, then, like pins, the lightening burrowed into my skin. "Hey, that tickles." I hated tickling.

The soft feeling turned to heat, turning my blood to heated lava. I swiped at the sudden sweat on my brow. I wrapped my arms around my middle and held on tight.

This is for Hyali.

I kept that chant in my head. I took my attention for every nerve in my body igniting, firing off as I jerked spastically. Whatever burrowed inside brought my body to life.

I could win any Spartan competition, climb Mt. Everest without equipment, anything. The electricity moved through my limbs, creeping from forearm to bicep. Foot to calf to thigh, warming my insides until I thought I'd combust. It settled around my heart, then sunk lower, until a warm full feeling under my navel.

I splayed my fingers across my middle. This was so not good.

A baby?

I hadn't signed up for this. But did I really know everything? In hindsight, maybe a few more questions were in order. There was only thing to say as black danced before my eyes and I fought for consciousness. "Liar!"

Mature or professional?

No.

But it was the best I could do.

Jumper

HE OPENED HIS EYES AND TENSED, waiting for the twerps to attack.

They did that whenever he landed in a new place. On cue, tiny lights appeared. He didn't know what they were. Like wasps from a disturbed nest they buzzed and twinkled, then dove at him from every direction. Jelly-fish tendrils, beautiful and distracting, packed a sting that made his nerves jump with each touch. They reminded him of his little sister, persistently annoying, painful, but bearable.

This time.

Each place they grew stronger. But this time they seemed content merely to pester with a few blistering touches, soft as kisses, then spinning away, most likely to annoy someone else.

He surveyed the world he'd entered. He never knew where he'd wake up. Each place so different and strange he knew it as a different world—if his mind allowed him that thought.

One place, he'd found himself face down in the dark hummus of a jungle floor, spitting worms that thought him dead.

In another, he woke in a tree that slapped him awake with leaves coated with acid. He'd watched his skin melt from his fingers before the pain took him to a new place.

This time, he found himself in in the middle of a shadowy street that rippled and moved beneath him like water under glass. Incorporeal figures—men, a goat looking human, fauns he thought they might be called, and an octopus with a purse in one hand, high heels and a parasol. They surged around him, and through him, going about their incomprehensible business.

He shuddered and tried to step aside as a woman pushing a carriage ambled past. His hand brushed the downy head of the infant with an elephant nose. It looked up at him and giggled as his arm passed through the top of the sun cover.

Sun?

He raised his face to the sky. A gray film covered the atmosphere. It rippled and twisted. Water above and below, held back by a thin layer. He reached up as though to do it himself. Like the urge he'd had as a boy to pick at a scab and watch it bleed.

He jerked back. "Don't lose focus, Phil. Find the target."

He scanned the shadowy crowd for a clue.

She had to be here, always one step in front of him. She left signs of her presence at each place, the imprint of a heel, the jasmine scent of her favorite perfume, a mocking reminder of her skill at jumping.

She would never pause to gawk as he did, he knew with certainty. She just knew too much. Did the twerps attack her, or did she move between the worlds immune to their stings or above their notice?

Each place seemed right for her somehow, somewhere she would feel at home, a part of that new place but different. She always appeared different and before he could recognize her, she would jump again.

Even now he didn't understand how it happened. Just that he jumped. Always the quest to find her. Doomed to chase, never to catch.

There.

A flash of red in the colorless world. A dress swirled in the mist, so much more real than anything else he'd seen yet. He leaped into action. As though drawn to his movement, the twerps attacked. This time he shook them off, heading for the shop she'd entered.

He took no notice of the sign as he plunged through the door. He drew up sharply. A lingerie store. She knew he wouldn't come in here. This had to be a test. She'd do that. Ask him to go into Victoria's Secret. He'd never enter, standing stiffly outside while she made her purchases.

"But I'll model them for you," she teased.

"No, you go ahead. I'll just sit in those massage chairs over there."

She'd laugh over the hurt in her eyes, but he didn't belong in there.

This time she stood near a rack of shadowy bras with a headless manikin with four breasts modeling something with polka dots. He couldn't control the thought that popped into his head. She'd look good in that. He turned, attention diverted again. In fact, even with all the color drained like a corpse from the fabric of this silent world around him, she'd look perfect in everything here. Why hadn't he come in before?

"Philip?"

He forced his attention back to the emerald eyes that studied him, a slight frown crinkling the corners of her perfect features. Like the crimson dress, she stood before him in full color, thrumming with such life he felt spectral beside her. Somewhere in the back of his mind it came to him that with each jump, each new place grew grayer, the life more varied, but lacking somehow.

Not so with her. He reached for her, knowing if he could just hold her one more time he would be saved.

She stepped out of his reach. "What are you doing

here?"

"I told you I'd follow you?"

She sighed, her breath stirred the mists, changed them, giving them life for the briefest of moments. "Did you?"

The question hung between them on the racks of slippery night clothes and bits of leather dripping chains.

In that instant he knew she would jump again. He lunged. Desperate to hold her to this place and time. She slid through his fingers. He fell into the blackness between the worlds, screaming as it ripped him apart.

★★★

This trip passed in the time it took the pain to fade. Eyelids fluttered, then widened as hazy shadows sharpened to life. He cursed.

Not the damn car again.

It always came back to this, never predictable as to when, but the one spot he pinned down as the place where he'd screwed it up.

She laughed beside him. Her hand stroked his thigh. He eyed the finger he wanted to see his ring on. The one carat marquis diamond he'd picked out would look so good there.

The movie had been a science fiction thriller. She loved sci-fi, he the thrill. Perfect for the both of them. He studied her, dismissing the straight stretch of highway he drove several times of a day. The line of her throat as she tossed her hair tempted him. He reached out, moving a wisp clinging to her cheek. Always so soft. He loved running his fingers through the long strands, touching her skin.

As though sensing his somber mood, she turned back, eyes soft in the dash lights. "Would you do it?"

"What, Baby?"

"Follow me like Hulley followed Claire in the movie?"

He touched her chin. "You know I don't get into all that hereafter stuff, Babe." He paused. Just like always, that sinking feeling filled him. It was the pause that damned him. "You know I love you, right?"

The light in her eyes faded. Her smile slipped. She nodded but turned her face so the hair slid against her cheek and hid the rest of her expression. "I know you do, Philip. But you are wrong. So wrong."

He tried to laugh, hating the way she flinched at the harsh sound, wishing he could change it. He tried to distract her attention. "Hulley was crazy—killing himself every time. And the sad thing is, he missed each time. She was never where he was, only signs. They spent eons apart. For what?"

"For love."

"What good was that? They got to see each other just the one time. How could that be love? They both had families, grew old—with someone else. He was really a stalker, just through time."

She did laugh at that, but the darkness lingered. An invisible wall he'd never felt before. "Maybe the love was enough," she said.

The air in the car shimmered. The red dress rippled, her body thinned and stretched. He reached for her, when he blinked, she disappeared. She'd made her first jump, leaving him stunned and alone in the car. His leg still tingled with the warmth of her hand, but no one sat beside him.

Bile burned his throat as he realized what had just happened. He drove her away with careless words and nonchalance. She'd tried to warn him. In an instant of absolute clarity, he knew how much he loved her, needed her.

A faint trail of dust motes sparkled in the lights of an oncoming car, the constellation of the woman who sat there a second before. A star map of the worlds now separating them.

The longing to scream after her "I'll follow you anywhere" consumed him, but as soon as the fire of emotion flared to life, fatigue smothered it. Crushed him.

The interior of the car faded to scratchy wool gray, rubbing at raw nerves. Eyes drifted closed, mind stretched, his body faded into transparency, a piece of shrink wrap pulled to its limits. The fate of the shadow creatures awaited him unless he found her, touched her, wrapped himself in her again.

A thought. A whisper of the word 'ghost' flitted through his mind. He grasped it then shook it away. A monotonous beeping pulled his attention.

The twerps.

Once again, they stalked him, just when he focused on a jump. They seemed to sense it, to stop him from following.

They attacked.

He yelled, thrashing in the grip of the tendrils. They were stronger now. He fell to his knees, gasping for breath, clutching. His fingers caught, held, then slipped.

He rolled, straining for that glimpse of red in the shadow world to guide him away, the clue to where she had gone next.

Like the first pink of dawn sun through the haze of smog over a city, it gave him the strength to crawl away. She still had the dress.

A beacon of her love for him.

★★★

He handed her the box. "Happy Birthday, Baby."

She took it, eyes alight. Payment enough for the time it took the clerk to wrap it. She touched the stiff, gold bow. "Thank-you. It's beautiful."

"You have to open it, Doll."

She grinned. "No. I like it just like this. You give me too many things."

I'd give you anything, he wanted to say. The words died on his lips. He tickled her side. "Open it," he growled.

"Okay, okay. Pushy." She sunk into his hand.

He fit the curve of her body into his, chin resting on her shoulder where he could breath in her scent. Jasmine and something just a little different that drove him crazy.

She lifted the glittering lid. "Oh, Philip."

He kissed her neck. She never called him Phil, only Philip. He loved the way it rolled off her lips.

"Try it on."

She did. It clung to all the right places and flared at her knees.

She wore it that night to the movie.

He might have been jealous of the way the men stared, but when she touched his hand, her eyes devoured him with promises of the night to come.

Then he'd gone and messed it up.

★★★

This time she waited. He gasped on the ground. Twerps finally gone.

"You don't belong here, Philip."

"I told you I would follow you." That sounded so cheesy, like a line out of that movie.

"You said you didn't believe."

"I was wrong."

She crouched, bare feet in thick blue fur—it stretched out and away. Grass on a rolling prairie with a sky of gold. She fit this world. A part of it—unlike him.

He lifted a hand to caress that soft cheek. His fingers passed through skin and bone with no resistance. He stared at the wisps of his fingers. Disbelief.

Too late. He'd found her too late.

She sighed. "Oh, Philip."

"Mia? Don't jump. Stay. Stay forever."

"I can't. You can't. Go back, Philip. This isn't for you."

He faded, stretched, that ripping just before a jump. His. Not hers. This time he would leave first. He fought, imagining himself bone and iron.

"I will follow you," he yelled. "I will."

Before the darkness came, the glitter of her smile filled his sight.

★★★

"Hit him again!"

The beeping of the twerps filled his ears, burrowing into his skull with laser precision, shattering the thought that would pull him to her again.

He screamed.

The sound echoed back in a sonic wave, silent, destructive, rending his sanity.

"Clear."

The little buggers struck with their highest voltage yet, ripping a gasp from his soul. His heart screamed as it surged upwards as through trying to escape his chest. His skin burned. The twerps sang annoying and disingenuous. Once sporadic, now with the steady beat of a bass drum.

"Watch him carefully." Now the twerps were talking? Someone higher and over to the left. But darkness surrounded him. It was the first voice he had heard, besides Mia's, in what seemed like forever. It lacked her even tones, scrapping across his ears like a knife on toast.

He hated toast.

"Watch him carefully. He almost got away that time."

So now he was a prisoner.

"How many in the car?"

How could they know about the car? Did they have Mia as well?

"Just the one."

The hand around his heart released. They didn't know. She'd escaped.

"It's been touch and go since he arrived."

Philip slit his eyes against the bright light and groaned, wanting to see who held him and how best to escape.

"He's coming around, Doctor."

Philip groaned. "Mia."

"Who'sMia?

"When they found him, he was babbling about another passenger. A woman. But no one can find out anything."

"No clues in the car?"

"Nuh. A purse is all, empty except for some makeup. His friends waiting outside said he quit hanging out. No one remembers a girl, though."

"Weird. Cross dresser?"

"Maybe."

Philip shut his eyes, seeking her face, a point of reference for the next jump. He ignored the rushing in his head and the babble spinning above.

There had been more than one in the car. Mia. She had jumped just before he'd turned his eyes back to the road and watched the front end of his car crumple.

She had jumped, and he would follow. Just as he should have promised the first time. He cleared his mind, turning out the machine's beeping, the scramble of bodies in a too small room.

He had to apologize, make her understand he was serious. That he loved her beyond this life.

He jumped for the last time.

Sunshine Girl and the Troll

BY THE TIME EIGHT SUNS PASSED OVER THE CAVE OPENING, Karn formed two fuzzy notions.

One, his mother's hulk would never again provide food.

Two, he would have to eat his siblings.

They lay like discarded carcasses in the nest of bones and meal litter, moaning with weakness. He started with the egg first. He cracked it against the stone wall and relished the warm goo that filled both mouth and stomach.

Two days later the smallest hatchling lay silent. The female watched him rip the limbs from the body through blurry eyes, knowing the fate awaiting her. After three days he crawled to his sister. He liked her. Together they tortured the youngest as though knowing he had no future in their troll world. She lay still, shallow breaths sighing the end. He hefted a large rock and let it drop.

He left the cave, keeping to the trees, crawling between root and trunk. The fire of thirst closed his throat. At last his nose guided him to a small trickle in a ditch beside a packed trail. He lapped eagerly and once refreshed came to notice how good the trail smelled. He snuffled at the prints. The scents tickled his memory. The delicious smelling scent was man and the other goat.

Not knowing how to catch this meat, Karn settled into a nest of leaves at the base of a tree where the cradling roots and rustling leaves lulled him to sleep.

★★★

Ice crusted mud sucked at Ziga's ankles with each step. Winter neared. She needed wood and food. Waulter refused to provide more than a single, dry loaf. She who tolerated his touch better than his own wife. The path narrowed to a goat track, leading towards the lee of the mountain and her ramshackle shelter.

Once, she had been a blacksmith's daughter, in love with the mayor's son. Plague took both love and family. Without protection she turned to a less noble profession than wife. Now, every winter she faced near starvation a mile from those she once named friend.

The dry crack of icing leaves drew her eyes to the ancient roots of an oak and a small body huddled there.

"Hey, child, wake up and go home. A storm is

coming." The form turned, blinking large, black eyes over a bulbous nose and thick, gray skinned body. A boy—maybe—certainly one of the ugliest she ever beheld. Given a thatch of blond hair it could fit it with Waulter's snot nosed brood. "You there, who's your family?"

She reached for his shoulder, but he cringed away. "There now," she crooned, "I won't hurt you." She looked down the trail, pulling her thin shawl closer. Few lived this far from Bifeld except for the hermit, Cay. She eyed the child, assessing. Her pretty face hid a quick mind where even now a plan coalesced.

She reached out again. "Come, Child. In the spring you will be Waulter's newest brat."

★★★

Karn nuzzled the warm flesh. It smelled like meat his mother brought, the good kind. He bit, relishing the squirt of blood. The creature grabbed him by the scruff of his neck and shook him until his tooth rattled.

"There will be no biting, ya here? I'll take a strap to you, I will." The words meant nothing, but the fierce gaze reminded him of his mother, and he submitted.

"There now. I think will we get along just fine."

The winter nearly took them both. Hunger and cold shred the flesh from their bones. Karn longed for his warm cave and he huddled before the tiny fire in the arms of the new mother. She often spoke, teaching him her words. By spring he knew father was Waulter. The woman, Mother. And not to eat the scrawny creature in the corner that blatted miserably.

In the spring, instinct guided him to grub for worms and roots. He brought them to Mother before green blushed the lower meadows. She made terrible faces, but they lived.

★★★

Karn barred his teeth at the pointing finger.

"That thing is not mine," Waulter proclaimed.

"Of course, it's yours. Looks just like your other brats save the hair." Mother stepped closer. Everything, from the tenseness of her shoulders to her rapidly beating heart was the most aggressive Karn had ever seen. "You'll support him, or I will go to the mayor."

Waulter stared hard at Mother. Then, as though decision made, reached for his belt knife. Karn attacked. He grappled Father's thick tunic then he bit the man's fingers until blood filled his mouth. Father screamed for Mother's aid. She lent it but did not chastise Karn. Instead, she patted his head with a small smile.

She jerked her chin towards the forest. "The next time you return—bring food."

The man stumbled down the path, grumbling and shaking his bleeding hand. Mother waited until he passed from sight before sinking to the threshold. Every muscle trembled. Her ribs poked Karn where she held him tight. Still, she seemed more relaxed than ever.

"All will be well," she murmured, plunking him beside her. "We're going to make it."

★★★

Life grew better.

The man, and those like him, visited through the warm months. They brought fish, bread, meal, meat. Mother grew stronger and planted a garden seasoned with manure. It produced a variety of greens, which Karn did not like, but the manure drew worms, which he did.

He grew beyond all expectations. One day using a second hand hatchet to split kindling, the next wielding a double-edged ax. After two years he ducked to enter the house and took over the heavy work.

One of the men taught him to fish and gave him a line and hook. Another supplied a sling. Still another a whetstone and a lesson in tool sharpening. He cut and carried logs to the house—made it larger, stronger, snugger.

The winters grew pleasant. Mother wove fanciful tales of heroes and their ladies. Of trolls, and faeries, and men. She fastened him with a piercing look and said in her strong voice, "trolls are men banished from the light for eating man flesh, My Son. Never succumb to the temptation to do so." Ashamed, he nodded, for sometimes he remembered the taste of Father's blood with joy.

Mother taught him to care for the sheep—and allowed him to eat the weak. Under his care the flock grew. He ventured onto the mountain with the flock, crossing the

71

bridge to the high meadows with the village goatherds. They avoided him at first. He towered over them, his gray skin more like the old hermit's than their youthful blush, until the day he saved Sunniva.

On a day when the summer winds blew hot from crag to valley, he trailed behind the gaggle of herders, sheep, and goats. They were a pretty, merry lot—all flushed pink and laughing. The girls had packed baskets and put ribbons in their hair. They walked arm and arm, giggling and casting sly looks at the boys. The goats seemed just as frisky, proving troublesome to the most experienced and oldest herders.

The happy group skipped over the bridge spanning a ravine separating village from the high meadows. They ignored the craggy drop with the familiarity of those born to its beauty. But Karn paused, leaning over the rope railing while his flock browsed on choice moss between the rocks of the mooring. Crag and cliff, rock and ravine drew him as no soft meadow could.

He peered to where an eagle swooped amid roiling waves of the thrashing river thousands of hands below. A flash of light caught his eye at the center of the bridge. One sunshine haired girl, braids festooned with violet ribbons, leaned near the other end. He knew her name as Sunniva, for the boys and girls called it often. She was the first to be shown a lovely flower, the first to be given a piece of sweet bread from a dewy-eyed admirer.

"What do you see?" she asked. He dropped his eyes

away quickly. Perhaps one of her friends stood beside her, for no one spoke to him. She moved closer, swaying like a daisy of the lower fields. "Why do you stare down there so? What do you see?"

"There was an eagle," his voice rumbled like thunder in the upper passes.

Sunniva did not seem to mind and pushed against the rope. The fibers groaned. "Where?"

He pointed.

The eagle swung higher, riding the eddies and shooting for the sky. Sunniva's freckled face followed every move until he flew too high to track. "How beautiful," she whispered. "Wouldn't you love to be the eagle? To fly whereever you wished?"

Karn would be anything to stand beside this girl and watch her look him directly in the face. He knew himself to be ugly. Everyone told him so, even Mother who fed him and protected him. Many a gaze flinched away on the few occasions he went to town. Sunniva did not.

"What are you doing, Sunniva?" called one of her friends.

The sunshine girl thrust out her arms and turned her face to the sky. "I am an eagle," she sang, "I am going to fly."

The railing parted with the suddenness of a gasp.

Like a ray through the clouds the sunshine girl fell, arms wheeling in slow motion, primrose pink lips forming an O of surprise.

She did not scream, merely fell toward the void. Karn's mind did not react, only his hand. He reached out his arm, the overgrown paw capturing the flailing limbs with ease, hauling Sunniva to the safety of rope and wood. The expanse trembled as the village children returned, enveloping their favorite in desperate arms. She allowed the girls to usher her back the way they had come, frolic spoiled by the near catastrophe, leaving only the few herders staring dumbly. The warm thread of the girl's hand tingling in Karn's palm.

★★★

The tale spread as a leaf fire and the villagers warmed to Karn. His food was handed to him instead of thrust. His firewood and fish sold more quickly. The goatherds called greetings.

But it was Sunniva who warmed his heart.

She climbed the arduous mountain path and perched near his flock. At first, they did not speak. He brought her the tail feather of an eagle, an antler, and delicate skeletons of field mice. Then she chattered about the lambs and made him a blue bell chain for his neck. He wore the ornament until it disintegrated.

When the ice pricked wind swept from the North, Karn prepared the sheep for the long months in the barn by shearing. Sunniva appeared and lent her aid to rolling the fleeces with Mother. Afterwards, when the long golden braids disappeared into the forest gloom, Mother shook her head at him.

"You could do no better, Karn, she is pure light and you..." she smiled thinly, "Well, yer a troll, now aren't you?"

He took no offense, his mother often called him thus, but always in a loving voice.

★★★

Few men came to the cottage now. Only Waulter with his weekly offering. He glared at Karn and insisted he be outdoors whilst he visited with Mother.

Karn shrugged.

Mother only tolerated the sloppy man's visits, distaste in every word and movement. Soon, he reckoned, the nasty man would be asked to come no more.

He loved the steady rhythm of the ax biting into the wood and often cut while Waulter sat with Mother after a visit. Round stacks framed the door and those of the barn backing it where now in the coldest months, even the sheep found warmth.

"I don't like that boy speaking with my Sunniva," Waulter growled one day. "It's not right."

Mother snorted. "It's none of your business, is it?"

"It is. He's my son. She's my daughter. I have a say."

Now Mother laughed outright. "He is no more your son than that fish in your hands. Take your pathetic *hake* and leave. My boy takes care of me better than any man ever did."

Waulter mottled like a teat with mastitis. "All these years, you've lied!"

Mother shrugged. "Only for my due."

Karn let the blade bite deep and stepped back to wipe his hairless brow. In that instant, Waulter succeeded in what he tried the first time Karn had met him. He pulled his belt knife and jabbed it into Mother's breast. For the second time that year, Karn's hands acted without thought. He pulled the ax and let it fly. It cleaved Waulter's skull and pinned him to the log wall.

Karn rushed to Mother. She patted his cheek. "You are a good troll, Karn, but now you must run." She breathed one last time.

He backed away from the carnage, fighting the urge to dip his fingers into the blood seeping from Father's veins. The copper smell fed his memories. Realization set in as he stared around him. Images of his sister, Mother, and tiny brother from before in a cave darkened his eyes. An egg. Humans didn't come from eggs.

Troll!

Mother had not lied. She never lied, not to him.

"Karn!" Sunniva stood on the trail, an armload of late flowers drifting to her feet. "What happened?"

He tried to speak. After staring a long moment, Sunshine Girl needed no explanation. She rushed to him, her warm palm on his gray skin gone cold. "You have to run."

"I—"

"Go to the bridge, under it by the moorings is safe and dry. I will come when I can."

★★★

He made a home under the bridge, snug between the great rocks over the sweeping drop. With Sunniva as an advocate, the village elders allowed him to live if he no longer came to town and cared for the bridge.

The flaxen haired girl visited weekly, bringing bread and meat and his flock. If he were gone foraging on the mountain, she left a garland of bluebells near the cave entrance. He wore the flowers proudly. They played a game where he demanded gruffly. "Who's that trip trapping over my bridge?"

Sunshine Girl laughingly replied, "it's your Sunniva, of course."

He asked the question for many years until age turned her lilting voice to a croak and she no longer came to the bridge. He queried the goat herders, and finally, after long seasons passed between the sounds of men, the goats.

Through the long years, when the memory of a dainty footfall stirred him from his slumber, he demanded. "Who's that trip trapping over my bridge?"

At the end, only the eagles replied.

The Berserkson and The Queen

THE WALL ROSE OUT OF THE DESERT at the treeline of the Msitu Forest 30 meters tall, 1,000 kilometers long like a stone sentinel. More impressive than its size was the fact it had been erected by the Karr in a matter of weeks.

A barrier.

A warning.

With a destination in sight, the driver sped up, slamming Gareth's head into the ceiling for the umpteenth time in the two days he had been trapped in the transport with the nattering ninny. Thankful the armorer who had seen fit to plate his head with enough titanium to cover the hull of a battle cruiser, he turned to growl at the driver.

If anything, that made the driving worse. The smell of urine filled the small cabin. *Should have killed him when we started.*

Tailwinds of dust rose high enough behind the transport to alert every enemy within 50 klicks to their presence. Gareth sighed and shook his head, removing his shades to scan the area for heat signatures. Nothing more than the usual small desert rodent life. Good thing the wall had been quiet these past months.

Nestled in the shadow below stood outpost Alpha-82. His new assignment. He'd longed to see the wall since a child in basic training. For the son of first genners there was nothing but war and the native Karr had fascinated him.

A feline humanoid species, they kept to themselves in small tree villages beyond the wall. The males, known as Toms, were the only gender ever seen, and some had been captured and raised as scouts.

The females, queens, were a mystery. One that had him scouring news feeds as a boy for the first information that a queen had been contacted. It never came. When he reached sixteen his orders took him West to the Tuporock continent and the wars there.

Dragging his gaze from the behemoth shadowing his new home, he surveyed the three structures. Room enough to house twenty-five men comfortably, the self- contained atmosphere provided protection from the cumulative neurotoxin produced by the trees crowding the other side.

According to his orders only five men remained. Four marines and their captain. The medic, sergeant, and ten others had been killed in the last wave of Tom activity.

The hovercraft pulled slowly into the bio dome. Barely had it closed over them when the driver leaped out, unhooked the sledge, and took off again with one scared backwards look.

Gareth snorted. He *should* have killed him.

He rolled his shoulders, letting the tension and kinks of the last two days melt away. Although walls of stone inhibited his thermal imaging ability, he deducted the building at which he been so unceremoniously dumped was the one occupied.

Resting his right hand near his blaster, ax balanced perfectly in his left, Gareth approached the door. The sweet smell of Maruka weed wafted through the cracks. Someone was relaxing and no one on guard.

Sloppy. It may explain why there were so few left to defend the outpost.

He pushed open the door without a knock and stepped through and to the right, his back against the wall.

Four men played cards at a table in the corner under a heavy cloud of smoke, but it was the woman chained to the wall that held his attention. Clearly the most dangerous person in the room, she sat separate from the others cleaning a DRT—205, one of the largest hand held disrupters available to the army. She handled the ten-kilo weapon as though it were a toy.

She lifted her head at his entrance, vertical pupils dilating in the light from the doorway, ears flicked forward then back. She bared her teeth into a smile, or hiss—he couldn't tell—sharp points leaving deep impressions on her ebony lips.

Black hair fell in a thick mane from her head, blending into the pelt running down her back. Skin striped black and white was bare except for a leather dress of orange and white. By its bold pattern he assumed it was made from a vanquished enemy. Most likely a Tom.

According to captive Toms, Queens were notoriously intolerant of their male counter parts. No one had ever seen a queen. Now he knew why. Looking at a beauty like that could kill a man. Or at least start a war or two.

"Great, fresh meat for Claws. We ask for an army, they send an idiot," said one of the men in the corner. He felt the weight of their eyes, but his gaze never wavered from the woman's. She continued assembling the weapon, never once looking down, deft fingers a blur of speed.

"Ten coppers seys she guts him in as many minutes."

"Come on, Troyan. That's just mean after what happened to Julisson."

"Take it or leave it. She'll have the gun together in a minute."

"It's not loaded. You don't think the captain would give her a charge pack," the last voice wavered. "Do you? Anyway, she's chained."

"I'll take the bet." said a fourth. "Under ten minutes or you pay up. Julisson took a day."

"This one may be big, but he's stupid. You don't even

meet the eyes of a Tom without getting attacked. Let alone a queen. The wars on the continent must be over, the meat gets fresher and stupider each shipment."

Their words meant nothing. He waited, limbs loose, stomach clenching in anticipation of the attack.

With a snap she slammed the completed blaster down and leaped for him. He stepped forward, turning the ax flat against his gut. Claws struck with a sharp ping, scratching across the surface with a high-pitched squeal. The chain snapped taunt and she strained against it, standing chest to chest, meeting his gaze dead on at three meters. Fur bristled along her back, ears flat against the side of her head.

His gaze never wavered.

"Think you to challenge me, small man?" Her slightly accented voice slid along his spine. The hair on the back of his neck stood up. A nail searched above the blade and pricked through his uniform. A trickle of blood warned him of the razor edge that could turn dangerous. He tilted the ax so the blade kissed her skin.

"Challenge? No. Admire? Yes."

She strained against the chain. He leaned forward until her breath brushed against his cheek. "Do you admire death, *Sujaa*?" she whispered.

"You wear it beautifully," he answered in a growl only for her ears.

"Kat-tarina! Stand down!" a voice whipped across the small space. Neither Gareth nor the woman looked away. "At ease soldier."

Gareth grunted. "One does not look away."

"No?" she whispered. With a flick of her claws she ripped open his shirt from waist to shoulder. He didn't flinch. Mere scratches. She turned her back and walked away.

The captain stepped forward and finally Gareth allowed his attention to be diverted from the queen. "By the Ax, you *are* a Berserkson. You guys certainly live up to your reputations, don't you?"

At the captain's pronouncement the four in the corner scattered, leaping for their weapons as nothing had made them before. He barely spared them a glance. He should have killed them for their sloppiness within seconds of entering the room. He shook his head, always the delayed reaction.

How did these people make it on the front?

The captain frowned at his haphazard soldiers. "No one has faced down Kat-tarina. Except perhaps the medic that saved her." He shook Gareth's hand heartily but looked over his shoulder through the door. "Are you on your own? I requested a First-Generation Berserker and a squadron."

"The last fell at the Battle for Panterot. They sent me."

The captain frowned. "Very well then. Come." He led the way to the queen's table. He flicked his wrist at the disrupter. Kat-tarina took it up and tossed it towards the men cowering in the corner. Two caught it and fell into the others in a tangle of of arms and curses. The woman curled her lip in disgust, met Gareth's eyes for the briefest moment, then turned to where the captain spread a map.

"The Wall. I am sure you know the specifics, so I won't bore you with the details. Our mission is to map and defend the area. A task made damn difficult by the trees and the Karr who will not tolerant anyone crossing. However, four months ago a native Karr scout arrived with dispatches from five other outposts reporting a massive surge in Tom attacks from the wall. We were hit within hours of his departure."

"A spy?"

The captain shook his head. "I don't think so. I've known Yonoku for the five years I've been posted here. A homegrown Tom raised in captivity and loyal."

Kat-tarina's claws dug into the table as stared down at the map. "A *musaliti.*" She spat.

The captain ignored her. "Then, just when another attack would have finished us. They disappeared."

"Disappeared?"

"Gone. All the outposts in the trees, every Tom within two klicks as far as we can tell. We've sent scouts, but the few that make it back found nothing." He rolled another map over the first. A thermal image from the only satellite left by the colony ships. "Then I got this. I had to pull a few strings, satellites are about worthless over the trees."

Gareth stared at the image. The forest stretched further than he ever imagined. By the map it stretched over 13 million kilometers, at the very end was a huge heat signature.

Millions of Karr in a great gathering.

Kat-tarina leaned closer.

"What is it?" he asked. She jerked and blinked.

Her eyes were blue he realized with a start, and there was no mistaking the wonder in them.

"A *mkutano,*" she surprised him by answering.

The captain glanced between the two of them. "A what?"

She waved her hands. "A gathering."

"We can see that, but what does it mean?"

A shiver ran through her pelt. "A storm is coming."

★★★

Under the wall night fell as though shot. Gareth found himself ushered out of the small building where the other men gathered, and shown to one of the deserted structures he immediately recognized as the brig.

"The men will feel more comfortable if you slept here." The captain explained. His voice hard but slightly apologetic. Berserksons had reputations for volitale tempers, killing sprees, vicious attitudes all around. Regular soldiers regarded them more as mad dog soldiers like their fathers than rational human beings.

However, Gareth's record was stellar. He did not deserve an iron box.

He dropped his bag to the floor with a shrug. Every place was home as long as he had his kit and his ax. This was a little on the extreme, two cells faced the front door, solid doors with large plexi glass windows.

"They were escape pods from first landings gone wrong. Completely contained with seperate life support systems. You could survive a air strike in one of those. They also work well for... " he waved his hand and trailed off.

Gareth shrugged

"Oh, and lock your door. I turn Kat-tarina out at night."

Gareth growled. Like an animal. "But you keep her chained."

The Captain waved his words away. "It is only for the men. After she killed Julisson they realized Hunter's pet had claws." He regarded Gareth carefully. "She seems to respond well to you however. Only Hunter ever really connected with her before."

"He found her?"

"In the desert, nearly dead. Been attacked, raped, left for dead. Would have too if our medic didn't have a soft spot for all things furry."

"What attacked her?"

Again the Captain studied him. "A Tom we assume. She's never said." And the army would never admit if it were one of theirs.

"But the night belongs to the Karr anyway. Good night." He turned on his heel and left Gareth alone.

He stepped into the pod and tried a switch. One bulb came on over a cot that would take a miracle to hold his weight. A blanket and a pillow adorned the top.

On the blanket written in red was 'beserkson go home'. How sweet, they were expecting him. At the sound of a door opening he doused the light and turned to the dark.

Kat-tarina stretched in the dropping temperatures, pelt shining in the night.

She turned on her heel and ran at the great barrier, made a five meter vertical jump, and climbed at a rapid pace to the top of the wall. He jerked his eyes left and felt the telescopic lens fall into place. She paced, head turning left and right as though patrolling—or hunting something.

"Alright then." Gareth slung the ax into his belt and started for the wall.

★★★

She did not acknowledge his presence when he swung up beside where she sat. He waited in silence, drinking in each elegant movement. The curve of her neck as she watched the desert. The flick of her ears at the slightest sound. The flare of her nostrils as she caught every scent. Gareth jerked his eye to the right and scanned for heat. Nothing. She shifted subtly, her arm brushing his.

The touch of her fur caused the immediate reaction of sticking his tongue to the roof of his mouth. He crossed his arms to hide his discomfort.

No one touched a Berkson unless they were trying to kill him. He did not remember a mother, he'd been handed over to the army at birth to allow bother parents could continue their assignments. She had been killed soon after.

The softest touched he could remember was a cuff to the head, the shoulder slug of comrades. That ended too when he become the only Berserkson in a squadron. Reactions tended more towards cowering.

But this woman had no fear. Her eyes tracked the movement of the brush in the wind. But there was no life. He turned to face the trees, scanning for heat. Never had he come across a place so devoid of living creatures. Even a battlefield had more, scavengers quick to the scene.

Why did she not simply leave and join her people? She climbed the wall easy enough, escape would be no difficulty. "You were found on the road?"

"That is not the answer you seek."

Garenth began working what he knew of her story through his head. What would bring a queen, a never before seen creature, to live voluntarily with a despised race? What woman would tolerate being chained to a wall because the men feared her?

When she spoke of a storm her voice held a trace of awe and fear. Why did she not run from it as her nation seemed to?

Only two emotions could he think of would drive any one to such extremes. Love or hate. Kat-tarina didn't exactly look like a woman waiting for or seeking a lover. Not that he knew the emotion personally, but he'd served with enough men and women with moon eyes to know this woman was not afflicted with the softer emotion.

She was hard. Sharp. Angry.

"Hatred then," he said.

"Vengence," she corrected.

"The man who attacked you?"

"The Tom." She tapped her chest. "There were two. Now there is one." She touched her ear with an exposed claw. "Marked here forever. All will know him."

"Scouts?"

" *Wasaliti.*"

" *Wasaliti?*"

"Traitors."

Now she did glance back at the trees. The silver moonlight turned the leaves to a deep blue that seemed to glow. Furrows creased her brow in a frown. "He must come soon. Before the storm."

"What storm?"

She shook her head and stalked away along the wall.

★★★

Her vengence came unexpectedly two days later. Gareth sat on the wall, partial to the place since that first night, scanning. Not even a desert rat until a plume of dust from the West heralded a visitor to the camp.

Not the post officer.

Way too early and he should come from the South. The dust indicated a small traveler moving at a rapid rate of speed. He flipped his telescopic lens. An air bike. This meant a dispatch—or a scout.

He climbed from the wall and waited, ax in left, right near his blaster.

A calico Tom stepped from the bike, patting his vest and shaking the desert dust from his pelt. He caught Gareth's cold stare and hissed in annoyance, but he was captive bred, used to human's ill manners. Gareth never dropped his eyes.

The scout swung a stachel from the bike and moved to the door, bracing to push past Gareth. The Tom lacked the feline beauty of the Queen. Head squarer and flatter, eyes less golden—and this one had a split ear. Just as the Tom made to pass, Gareth reached out and blocked the way with the ax.

"Move aside, human," the male hissed.

Gareth reached to open the door.

"Not human," he countered. "Berserkson. And I wouldn't miss this for the world. You're just in time, the guys roasted a desert rabbit that got caught in the dome."

Like any male after a long, dusty journey, the temptation of fresh meat caused the Tom's guard to drop and he shoved thorugh the door.

All activity ceansed for a split second, then Kat-tarina leaped, claws out, a screech of hatred filling the small space. The men scattered out of her reach. The Tom stumbled back. The Queen spat in frustration as she writhed at the end of her chain. Blood dripped from the scout's face. The chain had wrenched her back at the last moment, turning what could have been a clean disembowlment into a a non-threatening wound. No need for that.

Gareth gave him a gentle nudge forward. "You should have killed her."

The scout stumbled with a scream right into Kat-tarina's waiting claws.

★★★

Gareth went willingly to the brig. It was his room after all, even shutting himself in while Kat-tarina's escort struggled with the enraged queen. Two had poles with loops ared her neck, one managed the chain. Even so, they fought to contain her.

He assumed that during her time here she'd been relatively docile, her superior strength and volatile nature tempered by the patience of waiting. Now she would suffer the fools no longer and she lashed out with everything she had.

For a woman that stood nearly as tall as he with the strength of two men, it was impressive. She grabbed the chain and tossed the human over her head, then turned her attention to the unlucky two who held the poles.

Gareth sighed, let himself out of the cell, stepped around the commotion to the weapons locker. He scanned the weapons until he found the appriopriate weapon. Someone pulled a blaster and nearly singed his hair with a wild shot. He opened the ammunition locker, located the cartridge and loaded quickly. A soldier screamed. Another cursed and took the other's place.

Fools.

He turned and shot her. He would not have them kill her.

Liquid gold eyes met his before she crumpled to the ground. He hoped that wasn't hurt he saw there or he'd pay for it later.

Shaking his head at the soldiers, he deposited the queen in the cell next to his before returning to his own. He eyed the last unwounded soldier locking Kat-tarina's cage.

"Don't bother to lock mine until I speak to the captain."

"Captain's dead," squeaked the human. "He was the second one she got after that Tom."

They both turned to look at the other three crawling around on the floor. "But why? We took her in, saved her life. Got her healed. Fed her. Everything." He turned dark brown eyes on Gareth and it hit him how young this last one was. Probably had never seen any real action before.

"He never should have chained her," he finally answered.

★★★

He dozed, but knew the moment she awoke. Not from a single sound, but the absence of one. He tried his door. Idiots had locked it. Drawing his knife, for no one would dare attempt to disarm him, he opened the handle and removed the tools he needed. The door opened in second and he proceeded to do the same to Kat-tarina's.

She sat up at his entrance and nearly toppled off of the tiny cot.

"Easy there." He pulled a blanket around her shoulders, knowing from experience the chill that came after a good tranking.

She hissed, but it was a token threat. When the shivers started, he took a chance and wrapped his arms around her, pulling her long body into his warmth. One hand stoked her head—he'd never felt anything so fine—the other on his knife—just in case. Too soon the trembling stopped. Her metabolism must match his own.

She pulled back and punched him. Stars danced in the dark, and he couldn't help his grin. Packed a wallop too. He'd never meant a woman more perfect. The woman packed a punch, and he counted it as a plus her claws had been sheathed.

"You shot me!"

"They may have forgotten your value as the first and only captive queen and killed you. Evidently you relieved the captain of duty."

"So you would keep me here?"

He tightened his arms around her. Just this thought! To say yes, to somehow keep this incredible queen, so soft and fearless, for himself. She stiffened in his arms, ready to fight. He forced himself to relax, to let her go. "You are free go whenever. It is dark now. The soldiers will not come until morning." He laid his cheek on her hair and breathed deep of her wild scent. "The night belongs to the Karr."

He felt her answering smile as she pushed him back onto the tiny cot.

★★★

The sun threatened the Eastern horizon as they scaled the wall, but night still hung heavy in its shadow. He offered her his knife. She took his blaster. He touched her face. She leaned her cheek into his palm, then turned towards the trees. She stopped. "Gareth?"

His heart jerked sloppily at his name putting from her lips. He lifted a brow, knowing she could see it despite the gloom.

"When the *dhoruba* comes, do not breathe. When it is over, the Toms will follow." She flung her arms around him, filling his nose against with that heavy scent that nearly drove him mad.

Then like a whisper she leaped from the wall.

★★★

That evening the storm came, but it was not one that he remembered ever hearing or reading about. No colonist's reports that he had ever read on the Karr mentioned dangerous storms, though he did recall the idea that every fifty years the Toms seemed to attack in force and take back more of their territory. He soon learned why.

It started and ended with the trees. From his vantage point on the wall, he witnessed the shiver of the roots, a vibration that loosened the ground and revealed the thick anchors holding the trees to the ground. Like a worm, the movement climbed through the great trunks, many larger than buildings he'd seen in the cities he'd passed through.

Finally, the leaves began an eerie dance, the noise like a gale. Then an eddy picked up the blue substance that seemed to line the leaves and swirled it through the air, composing different patterns, mezmorizing and beautiful.

A speck settled on his hand. He shook it off instantly as it bit into his flesh. Not dust or seeds. Animals—and they were hungry. He closed his mouth and flung himself from the wall.

★★★

Four days later, the storm passed. Gareth emerged from the self contained brig with a hard push agaisnt the door. The blue creatures had eatened through the biodome and lay in drifts about the compound. He poked at one with a knife, but they seemed more like lifeless husks now than anything dangerous.

He scanned the outpost for heat signatures. Nothing. The men either deserted or dead. He found the four soldiers in the command center, blast marks scoured the walls and the windows were shattered. The bones had been picked clean, even some of the weapons dissolved by the ravenous creatures.

He moved to the infirmary where the soldiers had laid out the bodies of the Tom and the Captain. Bones.

He tried the communicator and raised no response from the neighboring outposts. Following the instruction manual, he tried further out, as far as the small device would reach.

No response.

He determined that the death reached for thousands of square kilometers. He ate only what rations he had in the brig, it didn't look like the pests had left much anywhere else, trying their bites on everything. Even the blasters had scourings on them. He sat on the way and waited.

The Toms came in the night, as he expected.

The first males approached his position on the wall, hissing and threatening in their tongue. He'd chosen the spot where they had said good-bye, as good a place to die as any.

When the investigation teams came later they would find his body filled with the wounds of his enemy, he would go down facing them, and his name would be recorded under his father's as a true Beserkson. But the attacks never materilized.

A fine Tom of bold stripes and white patches approached low, claws outstretched. It took a breath to hiss, then paused, sniffed, straightened, then leaped over the wall. The others followed. None paying him any mind except for the occasional hiss.

He tried changing positions, leaping towards them, swinging his ax.

"Come on," he yelled. But the waves of Toms simply avoided him and went on. He shrugged and sat to watch, expecting any moment a knife in the back.

Those that came too close sniffed once, then skirted wide of him. Grabbed his shirt and took a deep breath, and the smell of her filled his senses. He decided then that he may shower, but his shirt was never getting washed.

Five nights later he had sighted over 50,000 Toms pass over the wall for the length that he could see. They came in well organized squadrons each under the command of a queen. Once he thought he spotted Kat-tarina and started to walk to where the proud figure took position on the wall over two kilometers away to watch her soldiers cross.

At the last moment he jerked his telescopic lense into place. A blue merle with icey yellow eyes met his over the distance. The disappointment nearly knocked him from the high wall. He should have kept her.

Kat-tarina would have stopped, he told himself, if she came over the wall. He waited, but she did not come. Finally, when the flow of Karr seemed to ebb, he packed his kit with more ammunition than rations and strapped it to his back.

He gripped the ax with his left, right on his blaster, and turned his face from the wall and set off into the forest.

He *would* find her.

Of Weak Men

"**NURSE. COME FIX MY PILLOWS!**" Leona Marion Moore Gregory filled her command with as much contempt her 96-year-old voice could muster. She had few pleasures for one as old as she, but money ensured she had servants, and she enjoyed torturing them.

The new nurse, Lisa something-or-other, left the window where she seemed to be entranced by the gathering storm. Obediently she helped Leona sit forward, adjusting the pillows until the pain along her bent spine eased.

"Water."

Once again, the nurse helped without comment. Leona found it strange. Overall her nurses tended to be chirpy harpies driving her to dismiss them within a few days. This one had a different air. Not just because of her coffee and cream skin color, but because this girl's eyes shone deep, strong. Reminded her of herself.

A bang on the roof drew their eyes upwards. "The storm is building," the young lady commented at last.

Leona waved the remark aside, uninterested in listening to any besides herself. "Has my great grandson arrived yet?"

"No. But you said he would not come until later."

Leona gestured proudly at the array of pictures on the mantle. "He is the most handsome of all the Gregorys, don't you think?" Not that she cared what the nurse thought.

"I wouldn't know, Ma'am."

"Why wouldn't you? Look at them. My husband, my son and grandson, then Adam. Handsome devils all, but Adam beats them by far."

The nurse wandered toward the collage. "I don't know," she mused. "This one is very good looking, in a stiff sort of way." She held a picture up. "Your husband?"

Leona leaned forward. "Yes. Thomas Ian Gregory the third." She let her mind drift back over the near century of her life and the men that had passed through. "Handsome? Oh yes, but weak. So weak."

The nurse replaced the picture and came to sit by the bed, leaning forward eagerly as though sensing a change in Leona's mood from her usual sour disposition.

"He never listened to me. Defense stocks, I told him, energy, manufacturing—the backbones of our country. He wanted to speculate. Gamble. I let him, of course. The 1920s were not like they are now.

A woman respected her husband. Not that I didn't

have my own money. He did his thing. I did mine. He lost everything on Black Tuesday. Put a bullet in his brain before I could stop him. The police were very understanding, especially the detective on the case, and I made sure I was carrying Thomas' son that night."

Lisa Whatever snorted. "You slept with the officer?"

Leona shrugged a frail shoulder, ignoring the pain in her ribs, warming to her story. Oh, how she had despised Thomas. So weak, willing to follow instead of lead. With his background he should have been President. He only wanted his cigars and a charming wife who conveniently faded in and out of the background.

The memory of the detective's eyes still burned her, staring into her soul as he turned to leave. She almost called him back.

Almost.

"Theodore Ian Gregory was born nine months almost to the day that Thomas died. Well within the respectable time frame, of course."

A smile played at the corners of the nurse's lips. "Of course."

"A necessary deception. Besides, Theodore was mine, a Moore, even though he had the Gregory name." She frowned, remembering. "He might as well have been Thomas' though."

Lisa retrieved one of the newer pictures. "Is this him?"

Leona nodded.

"A soldier?"

Leona sighed. "Such a patriotic boy. He lived in the stories of World War II. Such an active imagination too. He made up a whole story of his father being killed at Normandy Beach, and had the whole school believing it, I might add. They were going to have him carry the flag in the Veterans Day Parade until I set them straight. He never forgave me for that. Fought me on everything. When I found him a wife, he didn't want to get married."

"But he did?"

"Of course, he did. Susan Nellie Whitaker was the perfect match, both for him and our business interests. Good family. Railroad stocks as part of her dowry. Not much to look at, but she'd been raised right."

The nurse gave her a sly smile.

Leona wanted to slap her, but it was obvious Lisa followed the story, not just the vocal one, but all the nuances underneath. Even now she could hear Theo yelling he would never marry the blue-blooded ninny.

Her own shouts that she would see him cut off echoed back.

He would be a soldier, he retorted, he didn't need her, her money, or all the strings that came with being a Gregory. She slapped him then. It had been enough.

"You will marry Susan," she hissed. "And when you get her with a Gregory heir you can run off and play soldier."

"You blackmailed him? How?"

"Blackmail? Never. I made a trade. An heir for a soldier. He married her. Two months later had her pregnant, then off to war." The funeral was magnificent, complete with distraught wife holding the newborn Patrick."

"He died in Vietnam?"

"Yes."

"What happened to the baby?"

Leona's mind drifted. Susan had been an attentive mother, but too permissive. After loosing two men, Leona believed her leniency caused the problems with the men in her life.

Perhaps if she indulged them less they would have been stronger. She allowed her philandering husband his illusions. Theodore his fantasies. She gave him everything. Too late she saw the danger. Susan would not be allowed to make the same mistakes.

"It was easy to take the boy. She was unfit to be his mother. She finally remarried and disappeared. She died later. I let Patrick think she abandoned him. To make him strong."

"But?"

"But the fool fell in love."

The nurse snorted. "Don't we all."

Leona's eyes flashed. "No. Gregorys have no time for insipid feelings. We have money, we have power, and we will protect it."

"I don't think the men agreed with you," the nurse snapped back.

Leona stared at the woman whose voice had sharpened to a dangerous pitch. Her jaw clenched. What right did the chit have to be angry with her? She regretted nothing.

"No. They didn't and look where it left them." All gone. Only her and Adam left, the last of the Gregorys.

Lisa took a breath and leaned back, releasing some of the tension shimmering between them. The wind howled. Rain sliced at the windows. Leona bit her cheek, unwilling to continue her story.

"So who did Patrick fall in love with?" asked the nurse.

Unable to resist, Leona continued. It felt good to tell someone after all these years. "It doesn't matter who he loved. It mattered who he married."

"I take it he didn't marry the woman he loved."

Leona slapped her duvet. "He couldn't! Some girl from Alabama or somewhere. She was hideous."

"You saw her?"

"Oh, he was too smart to show me a picture of her. I knew he was up to something, so I hired a private investigator to follow him. That boy had always been secretive." So, unlike his openly rebellious father. No, Patrick kept everything covert.

"A birthmark covered half of her face. She was deformed."

"A port wine stain?"

Leona shuddered. "Never would I allow such a mutation into the Gregory family."

"Wait. You mean the family that wasn't really Gregory because you slept with a detective after your husband died?" There was no mistaking the laughter in the nurse's solemn face.

"Cheeky wretch. But yes. We had a standard to uphold. The Gregorys have been a force in this country since its beginnings."

"Perhaps you're exaggerating a few things. I don't think anybody outside of this city has heard of the Gregorys."

Leona allowed herself a small smile. "True. But that is how it should be. True power is the person behind the curtain. The demure wife behind the senator—"

"Ahh, the mother behind the grandson."

Now she understood. "Yes."

"So, what happened to Patrick?"

"He married as I told him to, of course. Janice Gail Stanfordson. The family was going under, bad business decisions some, but mostly just spending beyond their means, younger generations lacking the understanding of where their bread came from. Even better," she refrained from rubbing her hands together in glee. "They had a pregnant daughter. Like Patrick she was lost in the free love of the seventies. The one thing they had in common was their drugs." She shrugged. "Within a few years after Adam's birth, they succumbed to their habits. Janice walked right off that cliff out there."

"And Patrick?"

"He lasted a little longer. Like his grandfather, put a gun to his head one night at a party. The police detectives said it was a game of Russian Roulette. He lost."

"Evidently."

Leona gazed at the young nurse, "Yes, evidently. Why do you wear your makeup so heavy? A young lady should only use enough to bring out her natural beauty. It is almost caked on, especially around your eyes."

"Yes, ma'am."

Leona turned away with a frown. Tree limbs lashed at the windows. The storm rose into one such as she hadn't heard in a long time. But the Gregory mansion stood as a monument to the Gregory strength. Six generations had lived here, and soon Adam would come home to take his place by her side.

"Where is he?" she muttered.

"Perhaps the storm slowed him down. The road up the mountain gets treacherous in the rain."

Leona sniffed. "What would you know of it, girl? You have only worked here a month."

"Oh, I haven't worked for you long. But I've known about this house my whole life."

"What is that you say? What do you mean?"

The nurse smiled crookedly. "Everybody knows about the Gregory house. The mean old lady crouching above the city like a spider eying her next feast."

Leona gasped. "How dare you talk to me like that?

Remember, not only can I fire you. I can destroy your career."

"Yes. I know." The nurse checked the window again and sat back down. "Why don't you finish your story."

"I don't want to tell it now."

"But Janice's child was Adam, right? You raised him. He's stronger than the others, isn't he?"

Adam. Her pride and joy. Despite the rocky beginnings of a premature birth and the inherited drug addiction, he was everything she had wanted from all the others.

Handsome, no nonsense, ruthless in business, understanding family, power, money came before anything and anyone. He excelled in school, disdained low society, and made her proud every day.

Tonight, she would tell him how she had legally transferred the businesses to him. A step she never dared before. But Adam had earned her trust. The first. A man of strength.

The door opened with a bang, and a cold gust of wind made the fire spark. Her heart leaped. He had come. He entered the room with a smile, but his eyes did not seek hers as she expected. Her nurse riveted his attention.

He strode across the Persian carpet, steps determined, almost angry. The little chit rose to greet him, dark eyes wide in her too square face. Leona's heart stuttered as he placed both hands on her cheeks, thumbs wiping at the caked makeup.

"I hate this. You don't have to hide anything. Nothing, remember?"

The girl's eyes glowed. She caught him around the neck and pulled him close. "Adam."

He kissed her as though Leona were not four feet away. The short, fierce kiss of passion seared Leona. She clutched at the pain that had been gnawing on her ribs all evening.

"Adam. Unhand my nurse and come here. What is the meaning of all this?"

Her great grandson turned his gaze to her. The hatred staring out of the blue depths took her breath away. Lisa stood by his side, tucked protectively under his arm. The makeup he had scrubbed off revealed a dark stain in the shape of a heart next to the girl's left eye.

He started to speak. The nurse put her hand on his chest. He subsided, but Leona sensed the anger still seething just below the surface. She had never seen him so out of control. This sly nurse had corrupted him. She would see her disappear.

"What is this about, Grandmother?" The girl asked.

"How dare you talk to me so familiarly. You are not part of this family, and you will never be."

"Be careful," Adam growled.

Before her stood a totally different person than the young man she had raised. Tall and lean, he exuded the power she appreciated, muscles honed from hours at his favorite pastime of boxing.

Again, the nurse touched him, and he relaxed, keeping her carefully under his shoulder like a small bird. Leona narrowed her eyes. The girl straightened, no longer the subservient nurse that had fluffed her pillows and wiped whatever needed wiping.

She stood gracefully, strong in her own right. "Let me tell you a story. A story of a mistress who became a secret wife. One with a huge stain on her face, but the purest of hearts."

Leona's breath caught. It couldn't be.

"Patrick married my mother before he pulled that trigger."

"You are fired," Leona screamed. She shook her finger at her great grandson. "I will cut you off from everything."

The boy had the audacity to shrug at her. How dare he? "It is too late, Grandmother. Per your request, the papers have all been signed."

"And you can't fire me," added the girl, "I quit." Her dark eyes met Adam's, their hands joined to touch her stomach. "Besides. I have more important interests to look after now." She pinned Leona with her look. "A true Gregory, untainted by your hate and machinations."

Adam cast a flat glance at his grandmother. "What of her?"

The nurse shrugged. "I will let the agency know

Monday that I quit. She can take care of herself until then."
She tugged on her coat, cold eyes dismissing the bedridden
woman. "Maybe."

The girl turned and stepped close, leaning down until
her lips brushed Leona's ear. "You named them weak, but it
was you all along. A man is as strong as the woman at his
side."

A chill shuddered through Leona. She looked
desperately for a phone. It taunted her from a chair by the
window. She had to do something, anything. She would crush
them. There was still time. A pain seized her heart.

Its beat slowed then stopped.

Stay

THE KA'AN TERRPLANT ROTATED, giving Kandra a clear view of the ship hailing the station. She sat forward, trying to see through opaque windows highlighted in the light of the two suns peeking over Archib's horizon. However, the ship remained a mystery, sharp against the knife edge sharpness of the blackness behind it.

The voice came again. Deep. Distorted by distance and space. "Hail to the Terrplant. We have an engine malfunction. Requesting permission to land for computer diagnositcs."

The older model fourth class freight drifted closer. Smallest of the cargo classes, it had weapons designed for defense. From her reading, Kandra knew the tupe could easily be outfitted to different, more nefarious occupation than shipping trade goods.

She studied the detailed art of red and yellow stripes blending into a raptor type bird. The whole effect was a vivid explosion of colors, one rarely seen in the monochrome theme of her home. Unlike any she had seen on a ship before. Not that she'd had the chance to study any up close. It stirred her heart to soar through space, to explore the unknown.

"Who's that ship registered with, Ka'an?"

"A freighter with that designation is not in my database," replied the Artificial Intelligence Central Processing Unit, AICPU, and her only source of information for eighteen dull years.

Big surprise there. Every time a ship passed close enough to hack an unprotected inoframe and update Ka'an, her paranoid mother moved the terraplant into the shadow of a moon.

Her hand hovered over the button tht would open the bay door, glancing over her shoulder to be sure the maternal unit lurked nowhere near, dropping the lower as she turned back to study the ship.

Making up her mind, she slammed her hand down on the release before her mother, with the annoying third sense of the Reqwe, appeared and stopped her.

Eighteen years on this terraplant, as long as she could remember. Just her, Mom, and the animals. One more day and she would be loonier than the *mustok*, that lone water bird locked in the Ag section because it attempted to fly through the windows every chance it got. They were supposed to mate for life. Problem was, the mate died sometime ago, leaving the other behind to go slowly insane.

Like her.

The ship spun into position, and she gasped as the name came into focus. *Jammin' Jack*. A Jacker. She turned in her seat, ready to alert the AICPU of a possible attack.

Her mother burst through the door. "What have you done?"

"Don't bother me now," Kandra hissed, flashing enough fang to show impatience but not enough to get her killed. Fingers flew over the control panel. "It's a jacker."

"Why did you open the door?"

Kandra shrugged. "I got bored. It could have been a refugee shuttle." That was about as possible as her living the next twenty minutes.

Jackers were pirates, scavenging anything in space they could find. When not savenging, they enslaved—anything to turn a coin. At least, that is what mother told her. But Kandra long suspected her mother made tales worse than reality.

After years on Ka'an with never so much as a hail from a passing freighter, how could she know anything anyway?

Guns hidden by a retractable turret, rose, taking aim on the bay door with an indisputable message. If fired, the dock would be useless, and even though the terrplant was self sustaining, it would mean Kandra was trapped here forever.

Her mother leaned over her shoulder. She smelled of hora weed. She used that more and more lately. Kandra would bet her blaster it wasn't just for aches and pains anymore.

The *Jammin' Jack* moved in to dock as though sensing Ka'an's lack of defenses. The Terraplant had been built for settlers as a stage for the terraforming and population of the planet Archib below. The planet proved inhospitable to colonization and killed off the intrepid dreamers. Mother bought the place for a song. Unfortunately, there were no defenses to speak of.

And the jackers knew it.

Mother slammed her fist on the control panel. There can't be more than a few on there. And they're alone. They may be deserters from their fleet."

"Or a decoy."

Mother smacked the back of Kandra's head. "You'd better hope I'm right. Either way, they're boarding us. Set the gravity in the bay to normal, then reduce it in the hall just on the other side of the door."

Kandra's fingers flew over the panel. These orders were the first stage of defense and one of the only they had. She hoped the sudden shift in gravity would throw the attackers off by bringing them in floating and Kandra and Mother could then shoot while the enemy gathered their wits.

The hand that had smacked her just moments before landed heacily on her shoulder, claws curled in rebuke. They pinched through her synthetic cotton shift.

Kandra looked up into her mother's tense face, skin the color of new spring leaves pulled taunt. Lines she hadn't noticed before deep around her perpetual frown. When had her mother grown old?

"I'm sorry, mother."

"Too late for sorries. Suit up."

Without waiting for Kandra's response, her mother whirled and leaped from the room. Legs longer and stronger than Kandra's own half human ones propelled her from the room with the speed of an asteroid burning through Archib's atmosphere. She followed as quickly as possible, habit pushing her to meet her mother's high standards.

She tumbled into the hall with the locker of weapons and ammunition just outside the flimsy bay doors, floating to the ceiling. Never missing a beat, Kandra grabbed the hand holds and pulled herself to the locker. She flipped down, tossed off her slippers and pushed her feet into the magnetic combat boots. Next came the battle suit, weighing 50 kilos and heavy as the guilt riding her now.

She dove into it, zipped the pantlegs over the boots. Slammed the helmet on her head. A preset tune from *Killer Planets*, a human music group from the Humanitarre system, throbbed in her ear.

Her mother's voice broke in. "Turn that crap off, this is real."

Kandra reduced the sound, refusing to obey completely. If death stood on the other side of those doors, she needed something to go down to. The beat thumped through the earpiece. Her mother's grinding of her double rows of teeth sounded through the comm link.

Kandra ignored her, checking the charge on the blaster. Full. The ticked of mother Reqwe barred her fangs, and then jerked a hand up. Kandra hissed back, proud of the two-inch incisors she'd inherited, then walked along the wall to the ceiling, placing herself upside down, blaster aimed at the door.

Her mother faced the door square, both the lack of gravity and her phenomenal strength allowing her tolhold and level two blasters.

An explosion rocked the bay, sparks from the flimsy barrier standing between them and the intruders. The stangers had powerful weapons—too powerful for those Kandra and her mother wielded. She risked a glanced at her mother, but the other never swayed, determination in every line of her body.

Kandra tried to swallow through the fear lumped in her throat, breathing through her nose, out through her mouth, trying not to fog the visor. Sweat dripped between her breasts and she longed to scratch at it.

A laser, steady and round, cut a hole in the door instead of another explosion. Through the smoke and fire came a regulator—a device designed for exploration and making an area save to enter. Lights blinked. Warnings flashed on her visor. Ka'an's system was under attack from a trojan, a virus years newer and more sophisticated than the AICPU's anti-virus program.

Her mother's curse cut through the music. Kandra hung

helpless as Ka'an lost the battle and the regulator normalized the gravity.

So much for their surprise attack.

The blaster dipped and dropped. She turned up and reached for the button to release the magnetic boots and fell with a thump on her mother's shoulder.

The other woman didn't flinch, just hauled her up, fingers digging through the battle suit. "Through the door—to observation."

"How did they know?"

"Doesn't matter."

A hand reached through the hole in the door, a controller pointed at the regulator. Kandra's breath caught and she turned to run, ducking as the crackle of her mother's blaster filled the comm link.

A man yelled.

Kandra turned at the last door. Mother slapped it shut. Crimson blood, dripped from her mother's closed fist, splattered on the canvas of the white floor like Ciferat art from a school lesson.

"Mom?"

"Shut up and get ready to fire. There are two warriors. Shoot to kill."

Her eyes met her mother's blue one and for the first time in a long time, the other smiled. "I love yo—"

The door exploded in a rainbow of shrapnel.

Kandra screamed and jerked the trigger.

★★★

Dangerous levels of benzene and hydrogen cyanide set off alarms in the AICPU of the Ka'an Terraplant. The system rebooted, double checked the indicators that suggested the firing of carbon dioxide lasers, then started the ventilation system.

The levels were already set to adjust to precise mixture optimal for the human respiratory system. The AICPU scanned the main living area for the two life forms the sole function of it's existence was to preserve and protect.

Four biologicals showed up on the scan. Two dead surrounded by polycyclic aromatic hydrocarbons and blood fragments from the thermal destruction of organic tissue. The life signs of a third suggested immediate medical help was necessary for survival.

A Lorilian male that had not been there before Ka'an's system was attacked began to move in the viewing area that overlooked Yupik, the third moon of Archib.

Although not specifically programmed into the system for support, AICPU added vanadium to the atmospheric mix, pushing it through a vent closest to the foreigner. The response was immediate, brain function improving, the secondary heart rate accelerating as he became conscious and sat up to take stock of his surroundings.

Satisfied it still had two humanoids alive as per its fairly nebulous directive, AICPU turned its attention to the closing of the bay doors and attacking the CPU of the ship in the bay who's trojan had briefly overwhelmed the terraplant's system.

★★★

Kandra watched the Lorilian man sit up, unable to stop him. He seemed disoriented from the blast, a small line of azure blood tricking from his nose and head wound just above where his right ear should be. She could not remember if Lorilians had ears or if the blast had blown it off.

She had bigger issues.

Like the piece of shrapnel embedded in her thigh and the ever-increasing puddle of blood below the injured appendage.

The man, looking younger now without his darkened flight helmet and weapon, caught her eye. Her hand reached blindly for something close by to defend herself. Her fingers skittered across bare floor and touched the round edge of the stylus for note taking on the infoframe.

She leaned for it.

"Stop!" The single word spoken in three harmonizing voices halted her movement. She had read about the three vocal chords of the Lorilians but having spent her whole life on the Ka'an terraplant she had never actually heard it. Recordings were rare and carefully hoarded by the race.

The man approached on his hands and knees, seeming to grow stronger with each step. In three clicks of the moon clock he towered above her, much larger than when he slumped across the living area.

Whether from the fact she knew death was imminent, or from his mesmerizing speech pattern, Kandra couldn't bring herself to care. She slumped against the wall, tipping her head slightly and exposing her jugular.

"Here, put pressure above the wound like this." This time, the stranger spoke with only one vocal chord. Warm, calloused fingers guided her free hand to the wound on her thigh, pressing carefully above the wound. Tremors shuddered up her arm.

Clarity and the will to live returned in a rush. She needed to move, to make her mother proud. Her weakness had drawn him closer. If she could just drive the point of the writing implement into his neck, she could order the medical bot from the bay.

Her mind slipped.

Was it even active? As far as she knew Mother had never used the thing, relying on more practical knowledge for treating injuries. Her body fought her will, systematically shutting down as blood loss drove her into shock.

Still, she swung the make shift weapon weakly.

He batted it away with a gentleness that caught her by surprise. "Uh, uh, uh." The three voices sang before dropping back to one. "None of that."

She fought to focus, keeping her eyes carefully averted from the body of her mother slumped against the wall ten cubics away.

"Where do you keep the medical?" The stranger asked.

Kandra stared at the man dully. Why would he want that? He looked well on the mend to her hazy vision.

Still, she answered the strange question slowly. "Behind you, in the utilitarian."

He turned with the inherent grace of Lorilian warriors and strode to the panel that opened at his approach. "Got it."

He returned and dropped beside her on one knee with the clear box between them. "Let's see what we got here. Oops, you're slipping. Don't let up on the pressure." He adjusted her hands and then snapped his fingers in front of her face. "Stay with me now."

"Why don't you kill me too?" Her tongue felt like she'd swallowed a Churuta and her words slurred, but she felt the question needed to be ask.

Why would the partner of the older intruder, the other body in the room killed by her mother be helping her now?

"Here. This ought to help." The sharp sting of an injection briefly brought her brain to focus and she looked into eyes the color of the maroon rings around Archib. "Why should I kill you? My father made the decision to be a part of this war. The Fembats and the Malecurots started this war, but the younger generations can finish with a simple ' I won't'."

Her head cleared for good as the pain receded with the painkiller in the injection. She relaxed her hands, no longer having the strength to keep the pressure.

"Hey, hey, hey. Not yet. You're losing blood fast and we have to get these bleeders tied off." Gentle fingers pulled her face around. "Stay with me—Say, what is your name any way? Our parents didn't really introduce anyone before they started killing each other."

"Kandra."

The young man nodded. "I'm Ladrian. So stay with me a little longer, Kandra."

He worked while he spoke. Kandra kept her eyes averted from the growing puddle of crimson below her leg. It crept up her jumpsuit until she felt she was sitting in a puddle of hydro.

Whenever she raised her eyes, death and ever-increasing rings of blood around the other two bodies met her eyes. She lowered them to the head bent above her thigh.

His hair was black, lying in tight curls against her skull that looked slightly flattened by the helmet he had removed with his father and he had intruded onto Kandra's Terraplant.

"It's about sex really."

Her eyes widened at his words and she tried to pull away. Her mother had always warned her about men.

"Actually, it's about the lack of it. Sit still now. I almost have it stopped."

"What is?"

"The war. How long have you been on this Terraplant anyway?"

Despite the pain, she chuckled then choked off as those beautiful eyes turned up to hers and he smiled.

She looked for a distraction and found it in answering his question. "I was born here."

He raised his eyes to her bare midriff. "Oh. You're natural

born. Two umbilici. Nice."

Heat climbed her cheeks. As though sensing her confusion, the boy explained himself. "Egg babies are born with only one, that one connected to the yolk sac. Do you have any Derma Glue?"

Kandra rested her head against the wall. "Utilitarian."

"Right. You don't have to press any more."

She risked a glance down. Blood no longer blossomed from her leg. It was clean and held together by five clips. She fought for coherency. "Wow."

He single slurred word made him frown. "Let's see if you have plasma tucked in there as well. You lost a lot of blood. Good thing your mother was able to distract my Father, or you might have been hit directly instead of just with a piece of shrapnel. I'll be back."

With his absence, the loneliness of the room pressed down on her. The blood began to smell as the atmosphere of the Terraplant warmed to the daily occurrence of slipping into the shadow of the moon. The vent behind her hissed and warm air flooded her, fighting the chill that seemed to posses her finger and toes.

She moved her leg experimentally, gritting her teeth as the pain ripped up her thigh.

"Stop, stop, stop." The three voices called from the door. Ladrian hurried over with more single shot injections.

Kadran still squirmed. "Just want out of the blood."

"Here. Let's get this plasmabots into you and the clips out

and I can move you." The cold tip of the DermaGlue gun made her shiver, nearly hiding the ting of the injections. Strength returned as the bots began to replicate red blood cells.

"There. All fixed up. Where shall I put you? The Fuchair there?"

She nodded and tried to rise. "I can make it."

"Nonsense. I want to DermaGlue to set." Lean muscled arms slid around her shoulders and under her knees, then she was swinging through the air and to the futar as though she weighed nothing instead of four cubarts.

She looked down from a dizzying height. When the strangers had first opened the blast door, things had happened too quickly for her to assess much. The crimson eyes, strength, height—all traits of a Lorilian. This would also explain his confusion about being born versus hatched. According to her research on the very outdated infocache of the Terraplant, Lorilian's were monotremes, mammals that laid eggs.

Ladrian gently swung her to the couch. "Let me get you some liquid—a girl cannot live on plasma injections alone."

"Ask the Terraplant."

Ladrian raised his eyes to the ceiling. "Terraplant—"

"Ka'an"

"Ka'an, would you prepare a drink concoction of electrolytes and bio-sugars for Miss Kandra."

A single beep indicated the AICPU 's acknowledgment.

Three more followed shortly, a light on the wall near the utilitarian turning green.

Kandra pointed.

At Ladrian's approach, a panel raised, revealing a chartreuse drink with plenty of foam.

Kandra grimaced but accepted the mixture and took a sip. "What is this war you were talking about?"

Ladrian gazed at her for a moment, verticals pupils wide in the light as though he were assessing her seriousness. "You honestly don't know?"

"Mother never went into detail why we had to stay on Ka'an. We just did. And there is nothing in the infocache on a recent war."

Ladrian glanced briefly at the bodies of his father and her mother. A look of sadness crossed his features. "Let me take care of our elders and then I will answer your questions."

Kandra nodded and heat rose to her face as she thought of her callousness, leaving her mother to lie against the wall while she questioned the stranger about a war.

Of course, if her mother had told her more about how real the dangers were, Kandra might not have lowered the shields at the friendly hail. She might have done a lot of things differently.

While Ladrian rose and went about finding the cleaning unit and bagging the bodies for disposal, Kandra fantasized about meeting him and his father at the door with a readied laser.

Would her mother still be lying in a puddle of her own fluids? Would it be Ladrian there instead?

The cleaning bots took care of their business, right down to sanitizing even the microscopic particles and cleaning the air the carcinogens created with a carbon dioxide laser burned organic tissue. The blood off the Lorilian father and human mother mingled in a small area, deep crimson with azure, creating a purple puddle the disappeared under the ministrations of the bots.

"You have a pair of cerula!" Ladrian appeared from the hall that led to the planatarium.

She nodded. "Yes."

"That is so Terra. Gives milk daily? Protein?"

Kandra nodded again and laid her head back on the rest. More fatigued then when her mother doubled her usual daily run around the the Terraplant.

"The war, Ladrian, please." Thsis war had evidently brought these strangers to her doorstep. She needed to understand why it was her mother lay dead. Why a stranger would shoot her when he had been invited in.

Ladrian approached, his face growing more serious with each step. She'd read that using the name of a Lorialian was special. They responded differently than most species, as though their name gave other control over them. And he had given her his.

He crossed his legs and lowered himself beside her once more. His eyes scanning her face. Did he know she knew about using the Lorilian name? It surprised her as well.

"It's a human thing."

"The wars of the past generally are."

"And a female thing."

She raised her brows at him until he added. "And a male thing. Once breeding for procreation became unnecessary, women took control of the sex trade and used it ruthlessly. The Fembat movement spread from planet to planet. So of course, the males fought back, withholding whatever they had to procure what they desired. Needless to say, it created a lot of bad feelings until the females of many planets combined forces to form the Femincreed Federation and--"

"Don't tell me, the males did the same." She sighed and closed her eyes. "No wonder mother kept me here and refused to keep the infocache updated. It would have been very easy to filch the information from passing ships, especially the cargo units. But she never did. She would change the orbit of the Terrplant behind the moon so no communication could happen."

Ladrian nodded. "I kind of envy you. There are neutral planets of course—many. But the poison of the few has affected many of those. Even Kruxta, where we came from, was a segregated society."

"So why did you leave and attack us?"

"Honestly I think my father thought this Terraplant was abandoned. It was dark and the shields went down at our hail as many empty Terraplants are programmed to do."

Kandra grimaced. She'd done that. And then the ship had docked, and Ka'an's CPU had gone down in a cyber attack. But Ladrian was still talking. "Father had been looking for a place for a while. Away from everything. Pretty much like it looks like your mother did."

If only her mother had known. Would it have gone differently? Could they have worked something out? The Terraplant was big enough for a small colony, what difference would two more people make when there were only two to begin with?

Ladrian leaned close and peered at her face. "You are beginning to gain your color back. And least, I believe it is normal. You were a little on the blue side, you are more pink now. I think it will be safe for me to leave."

A cold shudder ran through Kandra. She struggled to sit up and make sense of Ladrian's words. The walls, once so confining when it was just her and her mother loomed large and bare, the cold surface of Yupik tso far away. What would it be like to be alone here except for the Cerulas, bots, and Kismet?

She had no ship.

She could never leave unless she changed orbits and hailed a passing freighter. But what if the same scenario as the one that had happened just moon clicks before happened again and it was her life blood being cleaned by bots? For 18 turns of Archib she had been never been without another being. One she could talk to. Fear almost froze her words in her throat.

Almost.

"Why?"

Ladrian turned from where he retrieved his father's flight helmet from the bots. "What?"

"Why leave? Why go back into the war? There is everything here."

He stared at her crimson eyes wide then a smile touched his lips. "Ask me."

She returned his smile. "Ladrian, will you stay with me?"

C.I. Chevron

ABOUT THE AUTHOR

C.I. Chevron is the YA author of Metal & Bone and Four Days to Fusion. She is founder and creative director of Multiverse of Fiction, LLC, as well as member, sometime officer, and web administrator of Northeast Texas Writers' Organization.

When not writing, she manages a business, homeschools her children, and keeps bees, horses, cows, and chickens on a small farm in NE Texas.

www.CIChevron.com

One Last Thing

If you enjoyed this book, I would be very grateful if you would post a review on Amazon and your favorite social media sites. Your support really does make a difference and I read all reviews personally so I can get your feedback and make this world better.

If you would like to leave a review, all you have to do is click the review link on the book's page .

Thanks again for your support,

C.I. Chevron